*Commander Kellie and the Superkids*SM

#2

The Quest for the Second Half

Christopher P.N. Maselli

Harrison House
Tulsa, Oklahoma

Based on the characters created by Kellie Copeland, Win Kutz, Susan Wehlacz and Loren Johnson.

All scripture is from the following translations:

The *King James Version.*

The *Holy Bible, New International Version*®. NIV®. Copyright © 1973, 1978, 1984 by the International Bible Society. Used by permission of Zondervan Publishing House. All rights reserved.

The *International Children's Bible, New Century Version,* copyright © 1986, 1988 by Word Publishing, Dallas Texas 75234. Used by permission.

The Quest for the Second Half
ISBN 1-57794-150-0   KC 30-0902
Copyright © 1999 Kenneth Copeland Ministries
Kenneth Copeland Ministries
Fort Worth, Texas 76192-0001

Published by Harrison House, Inc.
P. O. Box 35035
Tulsa, Oklahoma 74153

Larry Warren/artist

Dedication

For those
without families...

Contents

Hey Superkid!

My name's Paul and you won't believe the adventure I just had. Actually, I'd call it more than an adventure ...I'd call it a quest. A quest to find my parents.

To understand what I mean, you have to realize I've been an orphan all 14 years of my life. I've never really understood what it means to have a family or to call someone "Mom" or "Dad" or to come home to my own bedroom every day. Until I was 10, I lived at a place called "The Sawyer Orphanage," then I moved to Superkid Academy to begin my training with the Blue Squad. My friends there have been the closest thing I've ever had to a family.

Missy, Rapper, Valerie and Alex are my four friends in the Blue Squad, which is led by Commander Kellie. She's a great commander and between the six of us, we've been on some real adventures with God. He's always faithful to take us from one great experience to another.

But what happened to me recently was far from anything that I've ever encountered before. The devil was working overtime to keep me from finding any kind of answer at all about the whereabouts of my parents.

But thank God for the Holy Spirit—because He gave me a revelation about the covenant God made with me years ago. Sound interesting? It was for me. Read on and you'll discover everything that happened!

Paul

The Quest for the Second Half

"I'm a *millionaire!*" Missy shouted, waving a flashy, unopened letter in the air.

Paul grabbed the letter from Missy. "Let me see that..." He opened it up.

"Hey!" Missy scolded Paul. "Opening other people's mail is a federal offense."

Paul smirked. "It's addressed to 'occupant,'" he said. "And it says you're one of two *trillion* people who *could* win *if* your name is picked. See? Check out the small print."

"So I'm not an instant millionaire?"

Paul shook his head. "Not on this planet." Missy huffed a note of mock concern and continued to flip through her mail.

Paul, Missy, Rapper, Valerie, Alex and Commander Kellie were all relaxing in an empty storage room at Superkid Academy after an *almost* perfect surprise birthday party for Alex. Everything would have gone without incident, but then everyone *except* Alex got caught in an old trap, set years ago by NME.

Notoriously Malicious Enterprises (NME) has a sole purpose: to brainwash kids with fear and deception...and they'll go to any extreme to do it. The Superkids' goal, on the other hand, is to share the good news of God's Word with the world. Therefore, NME and the Superkids are certain enemies.

This time, to the Superkids' advantage, Alex had bravely rescued the others from the trap. And now they were finally able to celebrate his birthday. Paul looked around the room, smiling at his companions on Superkid Academy's Blue Squad. God had given each of them different abilities, different talents and even different personalities. Over time, Paul had discovered it was their differences that made them one of the best teams at Superkid Academy.

Paul had always considered himself to be the most adventurous of the bunch—and the other Superkids would agree. Somewhat rugged, but quick and to the punch, Paul was thought of by the others as a born leader. Quite frankly, that was fine with Paul, because he loved leading adventures—going into new territory and discovering the unexpected. From as far back as he could remember, Paul liked the daring and dangerous. Even the sports he chose—like vintage dirt-bike racing—proved to everyone he wasn't afraid to get a little dirty. Best he could figure, he must have picked up his independence as a result of his 10 years growing up alone in an orphanage.

Not having a family like the others was difficult for Paul. In fact, when he first arrived at Superkid Academy, he told everyone his parents were just gone a lot and that's why he didn't have a lot to say about them. Paul apologized later for lying and told his friends the full truth. Since then, he had dived into a leadership role and pushed most of his fears and feelings about being without a family aside.

Paul's natural leadership skills came from his strong spirit, which was the quality that made the orphanage highly recommend him for training...and the Academy was eager to give him an opportunity to prove himself. Nonetheless, truth be known, Paul only joined the Academy to have a "good time." In those days, Paul wasn't a Christian or anything close to it. But it didn't take long. The love from his new friends and a powerful encounter with Jesus on his first adventure left him hungry to learn more about living for God and sharing the truth of God's Word with others.

Now he was a welcome addition to the specialized Academy that trained kids—from all over the world—how to live powerful, anointed lives and victoriously defeat the enemy at every turn. By graduation, Paul and the other Superkids will not only be well-versed in higher-level academics, but also firmly grounded in the Word and fully trained in the latest survival techniques.

"Junk, junk, junk," Missy pronounced over each letter as she thumbed through her stack. "Junk, junk, ooh—a new beauty catalog." She put the catalog aside. "Junk, junk and ooh again! A letter from Mommy and Daddy." Missy always called her parents "Mommy and Daddy."

She carefully sliced open the back of the envelope with her thumbnail. She pulled out a check and waved it in the air, aiming close for Paul's face. "Check for Missy!" she proclaimed. She stuffed it in her pants pocket and retrieved the letter from the envelope. It was written on fancy, floral stationery. She stuck the envelope behind the letter as she read silently.

But something on the envelope Missy was holding caught Paul's eye—and when he realized what it was, it made his stomach tighten. Valerie was the first to notice Paul's face turning pale.

"Paul, what is it?"

Paul jumped up, spilling his bowl of ice cream on the floor. He snatched the envelope from Missy, almost tearing the letter in the process. "Hey!" she cried.

"Paul?" Commander Kellie looked on with concern.

Paul held the envelope up in the light and peered closely at it. Stamped on the envelope by the post office, a red postmark that read "★★★ NAUTICAL ★★★ SEPTEMBER 9" glimmered in the light.

"Paul, are you OK?" Alex wondered.

Valerie approached Paul and shook his shoulder. Paul didn't even feel her touch. "Paul?"

"You guys," he said at last, gasping for a breath of fresh air. "You won't believe this."

The Superkids all waited for an answer.

"Are you going to tell us?" Alex wondered with a smile.

Suddenly, Paul ran out of the room with the envelope. In the distance behind him, he heard Missy ask, "Did I just miss something, or did he just steal my envelope?"

Paul trekked down a familiar hallway of Superkid Academy and came to an express lift. Not taking his eyes off the insignia on the envelope, he pressed a button on the wall and the door to the lift opened with a hiss.

Paul expressed down to Level 3, where the Blue Squad dorm rooms were located. When he reached his destination a moment later, he dashed out of the lift and ran to his room.

Could it be? he wondered silently as he ran. *Could it be?*

He reached room 312, the large dormitory room he shared with Rapper and Alex, and the door slid open when he thumped on a nearby button. Clean dressers and precisely made bunk beds welcomed him. Paul dived to the floor and reached under his bed, struggling to grab hold of an old, off-white, cardboard box. His eager grip nearly ripped its flimsy handle as he pulled it out. He tossed off the lid with full force, pulled out a worn blue, white and gold blanket and headed back out the door with it.

Only minutes later, Paul ran back into the room where Commander Kellie and the four Superkids were finishing off their birthday treats. With a liquid vacuum built right into his shiny, metal body, Techno, the Blue Squad's robot, was cleaning up the ice cream Paul spilled.

"Paul, where'd you go?" Rapper put down his plastic bowl and utensil. "What's up?"

Paul spread his blanket out on a clean section of the floor. He unrolled the corners and held it straight, being careful not to stretch it. The blanket was about 4 feet long and 4 feet wide. Bands of blue and white striped the cloth from top to bottom. Embroidered in the middle, in faded gold, was a familiar emblem—three stars followed by the word "Nautical" and three more stars. Underneath it were the peeling, fabric letters "SA 17 36."

"Where's the 'U'?" Alex asked, pointing to the abbreviation for the United States of America. "And what's this—a postal code?"

"That's my guess," Paul answered. "The blanket's old. I think the 'U' and the middle number fell off. But don't you see?" He pointed to the gold lettering. "It's the same emblem that's on this envelope's postmark."

"So?" Missy wasn't impressed. "You got a blanket from my hometown."

"No," Paul corrected. "I got a blanket from *my* hometown."

"But you said the orphanage you grew up in was in some place called Sawyer..."

"It is!" Paul exclaimed. "But when I arrived at the orphanage, this blanket was delivered with me. I always thought 'Nautical' was just a brand name. I didn't realize it was a city. This is a *clue*, Missy! My parents must be from Nautical!"

"So..."

"So next week is our vacation week, right?"

Valerie piped up. "Yeah, we were all going to go visit my family on Calypso Island."

"Change in plans," Paul said, smiling. "You guys have fun...but I'm going to find the half of my life that's been missing...I'm going to find my parents!"

▲   ▲   ▲

That evening, inside Superkid Academy, a dim light crept out from underneath the door of Room 312. Inside, lying on bunk beds, Paul, Rapper and Alex talked about the day's many unexpected events.

Alex chuckled as he rubbed his calloused hands together and told his best friends the story of everything he went through to rescue them from the NME trap they had fallen in. Alex lay on an upper bunk, above a lower bunk that he had converted into a mini-computer station. Directly catty-cornered from him, Rapper occupied the bunk above Paul. He laughed as Alex recalled the story. But beneath him, Paul wasn't entirely paying attention. His mind drifted with thoughts of meeting his parents after 14 years as an orphan. *What would they look like? Would they want to see him? Were they Christians? Were they rich? Were they poor? Were they even alive anymore?*

"I'm going to find out," Paul muttered to himself. Rapper flung his head over the side of his bunk and gazed down at Paul.

"What?"

"Huh?"

"You said something."

"I said something?"

Rapper glanced up at Alex, who confirmed Rapper's accusation with a nod.

"I'm sorry, guys," Paul apologized. "I must be daydreaming."

Alex flipped on his stomach and bunched his soft pillow underneath his neck, planting his chin on the top. "It must feel strange to think you could find your family...and see them for the first time."

"I *will* find them," Paul countered. "I'm sure of it. But it *is* strange to think about. I've never had a family."

"It's strange for me to think about *not* having a family," Alex admitted. Paul simply nodded. He would have loved to have grown up with a family like Alex did. Alex was the youngest of the Superkids and the resident "computer brain." He was the shortest of the three boys, with dark skin and brown eyes. Alex once told Paul that as far back as he could remember, Jesus had been his Lord. He often talked about his brother and twin sisters, how they laughed together and teased each other— always in fun and love. His father would take the family to sporting events; his mother would prepare big family picnics on Sunday afternoons. It was so picture-perfect to Paul. Just thinking about it made him long for a family of his own.

"It *is* strange to think about not having a family," Rapper concurred. Because of his outgoing personality complete with spiked, brown hair, Paul never would have guessed Rapper's family had experienced any problems. But Rapper's parents divorced when he was 2. After their divorce, his mom became a Christian. Rapper was to follow, but not before joining a gang with his brother for several years. Since then, his brother had been killed as a gang member and Rapper admitted that he hadn't seen his dad much, except during holidays. Still, each day, Rapper prayed for his dad's salvation. "One day soon," Rapper would say, "my dad'll be rappin' the Word with me."

"I don't have any siblings anymore," Rapper continued, "but I can't imagine a Christmas going by when I don't see my aunts and uncles...my cousins...my grandma and grandpa...those are some of my favorite times."

"Are you guys trying to cheer me up?" Paul asked. Rapper and Alex looked squarely at each other and each of them shook their heads.

"Sorry, guy," Rapper apologized. Paul smiled.

"I'm going to find them—I really believe that. But what if they don't want me?"

"Don't think about all that," Rapper encouraged. "Remember 1 Peter 5:7—Cast all your anxiety, or worries, on Him, because He cares for you."

Paul nodded.

"Yeah, and remember, Ephesians 2:19 says we're all members of God's household. We're family—brothers and sisters," Alex kindly added.

Paul shook his head. "Thanks, but it's not quite the same."

Rapper sat up with a start. "Whoa-whoa, what are you saying, bud? Actually, what we have as the family of God is better!"

"Better than family sporting events, Sunday picnics and holiday dinners? I don't think so. No offense, but you guys just don't understand. You're not orphans."

"Not orphans." Rapper scratched his head quickly, like he was after a flea colony. "Not orphans. Paul, *I was* an orphan—and so was Alex."

"I *was?*" Alex raised himself up. Paul imagined he could see a question mark hovering above Alex's head.

"We were *all* orphans," Rapper assured Alex. Paul sat up on his bed, letting his feet thump to the floor. His left sock slowly crawled down his leg, exposing the tip of a birthmark.

"I don't get what you mean," Paul stated. Rapper hopped off his top bunk and dropped to the floor. He stood in the center of the room, as though he was in the limelight, and began to explain. He was wearing neon-green shorts and an orange T-shirt. Royal-blue socks highlighted the outfit. The bold clashing of colors made Paul wince.

"It's all about *covenant,*" Rapper stated.

"Covenant?" Alex said the word like it was strange to him.

"It's like a promise," Paul explained. "Only stronger. Once a covenant is made, it can't be broken, right?"

"Right," Rapper agreed. "I know about covenants because I was in a gang before I became a Christian. We had covenants. We exchanged our jackets as a way of saying, 'I give you my authority.' And we exchanged our weapons as a way of saying, 'I'll fight your fights and enemies as if they were my own.' Then we'd announce our loyalty to each other—even to death."

"How'd you get out?" Paul wondered. Rapper shook his head to indicate his regret about ever getting involved with a gang in the first place.

"I came to Superkid Academy. They helped me get out." Rapper paused for a long moment. Paul interrupted his thoughts.

"So what does this have to do with me being an orphan?"

"Well," Rapper finally said. "The covenant the Vipers made—that's the gang I was in—wasn't much different from some they made in the Old Testament. Right there in the Bible in 1 Samuel 18, David and Jonathan made a covenant. And in Genesis 15, God made a covenant with Abram, whose name was later changed to Abraham."

"Yeah," Paul said, remembering. "Didn't Abram kill some animals and walk between them?"

"This is getting disgusting," Alex muttered.

Rapper took the limelight again. "Sure, it sounds disgusting to us, but Abram knew that a Blood Covenant was the most powerful agreement that could be made—breakable only by death. When God made that covenant with him, Abram realized everything he had belonged to God—even his life. But also, everything God had belonged to him."

"Not a bad deal," Paul admitted.

"Yeah, and our covenant is like that, too," Rapper said. "When Jesus died for us, He made a Blood Covenant with us—remember, His blood was shed. Everything He has is ours, everything we have is His. Check it out, Paul: We were each orphans lost in our sin. But Ephesians 1:5 says that because of what Jesus did for us, we are adopted as God's very own sons! None of us are orphans anymore—not even you, Paul. You have a family now—us—the Body of Christ."

"Well, that might be, bud." Paul lay back down on his bed and threw his head back on his goose-down pillow. "But it's just not the same. It's a nice sermon, but this Christmas you'll be visiting your grandma and grandpa's and Alex will be opening presents at a reunion. Me? I'll be wondering why I couldn't be one of you guys. All my life part of me has been missing—half of me has been incomplete. I need that second half—a family—to make me whole. So I appreciate the encouragement, but I've got to search for my parents. I have to see if I have a family like you guys do. And even if I don't,

I'd rather know that than always wonder. I don't care what it takes. Tomorrow, I'm going on a quest—I'm going to find my second half!"

"The weather doesn't look so good." Rapper pointed to the dark clouds rolling in from the west. The noonday sun was bright, but was being threatened by the approaching, stormy weather.

Paul stood with Commander Kellie, Rapper and Valerie in a local tramport—a terminal where trams enter and exit, continually loading and unloading passengers. Alex was unable to make it. His father called earlier that morning, excited that he had won tickets to a basketball playoff game. Alex had planned on flying out with Missy, Rapper and Valerie to Calypso Island, but with the changing weather, it looked like their vacation would be put on hold. So, Alex decided to visit his family instead. Rapper was a bit disappointed that he'd be the only guy going to Calypso now, but when he considered the sunny beach and Valerie's mom's roasted boar, he quickly got over it.

Missy hadn't shown up to see Paul off either. A few hours before departing for the tramport, Missy told Paul she wanted to join him on his search. Paul thanked her, but said he'd rather conduct the search alone.

"But where are you going to stay?" she had asked.

"Probably the orphanage I grew up in," he answered. "Turns out it's not too far from Nautical. It's like a clue already, huh? So don't be concerned—I'll be all right."

"Why don't you stay with my parents? They live in a big house on the north side of Nautical. C'mon, Paul, I'll join you. It'll be fun. I can see my parents and you'll have a place to stay. I think it sounds like quite an adventure."

"Thanks, but no, Missy. I want to do this on my own. Being with someone else's family will be a constant reminder that I don't have one...well, not yet anyway. I'm going to find them, but I have to do this alone."

"Paul, we all need each other—let me help!"

"Missy, you just don't understand."

"I don't understand?!"

"You don't understand."

"Ugh! Paul Temp, you are impossible!" Then Missy stormed off and no one had seen her since.

"She's pretty mad, huh?" Rapper quizzed Paul. Paul was gazing out the window at the moving clouds.

"Yeah, she's upset. But I didn't think she was so mad she wouldn't join in seeing me off."

Commander Kellie put her arm around Paul's shoulder. "Well, when I see her, I'll talk to her."

Paul smiled as he watched a bird swoop by. "She'll be fine once she joins Rapper and Val on Calypso. I think all the excitement and trouble yesterday really worked her up." Commander Kellie, Rapper and Valerie nodded in agreement.

All four members of the Blue Squad were dressed casually for their week of vacation. The Superkid Academy squads alternate vacation weeks so that the Academy is never left with more than one vacationing team (except for holidays). This early autumn week, it was the Blue Squad's turn—and everyone was ready for it.

Paul, Rapper and Valerie wore bluejeans and athletic shoes. Paul completed his outfit with a black, white and purple rugby and a light-gray jacket. Rapper simply wore a dark green T-shirt and Valerie sported a flowered blouse and a fancy Blue Squad recreation jacket—royal blue with thin, gold stripes on the sleeves. Commander Kellie's lightweight jacket was the same as Valerie's, but her outfit was comprised of matching Academy slacks, a blue turtle-neck and flats.

A loudspeaker blurted out a gurgled, computerized voice. "Tram C-64 to Metro City and on to Nautical now boarding, Gate 25."

"That's you!" Commander Kellie declared. "Let's pray before you go." On instinct, the Blue Squad members joined hands and bowed their heads. Commander Kellie prayed.

"Father God, we come before You in the mighty Name of Jesus, by faith. Father, today Paul is searching for an answer and we thank You for giving wisdom to him according to James 1:5. Lord, Psalm 119:105 says Your Word is a lamp to his feet and a light for his path.

We stand on that verse today. Only You know where Paul's parents are right now and I send out angels to find that answer and deliver it to Paul. Lord, we pray that above all, Your will is done. And because of the covenant You made with us, we rely on Your strength for our weakness. May Your anointing lead Paul directly to the truth."

Valerie prayed next. "And also, we pray for Paul's protection. Father God, we stand on Your Word in Isaiah 54, which says that Paul will be safe from those who would hurt him. He has nothing to fear, because he goes to You, God, for safety and You will protect him. As Psalm 91 says, You'll save him from hidden traps and You will be Paul's armor and shield. We thank You, Lord, that angels are in charge of Paul during this trip. They watch over him wherever he goes. We agree together for these things in Jesus' Name, amen!"

"Amen!" Paul echoed. He gave each of his friends a hug and uttered thanks.

"You keep in touch," Commander Kellie said with a smile. "I want to know where you end up staying and how things are going."

"I will," Paul agreed.

"Lemme help," Rapper offered, moving on with Paul and grabbing his durable, gray footlocker. Rapper wheeled it down the hall. It wasn't very difficult to move since it had four, large rubber wheels—nonetheless, it was big, boxy and packed with Paul's clothes for a full week's trip. As they approached the flashing red gate, Paul stopped.

"Look, when you see Missy tonight, would you tell her I'm sorry? I know she'd like to help me and see her parents, but this is something I have to do by myself. I appreciate her offer, though."

Rapper nudged Paul's shoulder with his fist. "Solid with me," he said. "I'll relay the message."

Paul slid his boarding pass into an electronic slot. It punched a series of holes in the pass. "Thank you and enjoy your trip," said a female computer voice. The doors to the tram slid open with a loud hum. Paul entered, rolled his footlocker into a tightly secured luggage rack and found an open seat by a window.

Outside, Commander Kellie, Rapper and Valerie waved their goodbyes. In a moment, the tramport was a small speck in the distance and Paul was on his way to Nautical. Balking at the four-and-a-half-hour, 1100-mile trip due east, Paul, ignoring the other passengers, nestled down in his seat and fell asleep, dreaming of his coming adventure.

▲ ▲ ▲

Paul looked up to see a figure coming toward him dressed in a glowing, white robe. His face was bright, too—and his eyes were piercing, like a beam of sunlight reflecting off a polished metal surface. Paul felt a gripping at his heart and a force of peace at the same time.

The figure promptly removed his robe and traded it with the light-gray jacket Paul wore. On Paul, the robe glistened like no garment he'd ever seen. Next, the man produced a full suit of armor, similar to a knight's armor. He clipped the breastplate onto Paul, followed by the lower-body part and then the shoes. He placed the helmet on Paul's head and handed him a glistening sword and shield set.

"The agreement must be sealed," the figure stated, his voice booming like thunder. Suddenly, as Paul stood frozen, a rugged, wooden cross rose behind the man. Without even a blink of hesitation, he stretched out his arms parallel to the structure's crossbeam. Wearing Paul's thin jacket, he was easily bound to the cross.

Paul couldn't bear to watch as he saw nails appear in the figure's hands and feet. The man cried out, and Paul could do nothing.

Paul was speechless, but eventually the words came. "Why would you give me all this? Why are you going through this? Why—when you wouldn't have to?"

"Metro City," a voice answered in the distance.

"What?" Paul asked.

"Metro City," repeated the computerized voice. Suddenly the tram came to a halt, jolting the passengers. Paul woke with a start and realized he'd been dreaming. He wiped the perspiration from his brow.

Halfway there, he thought.

The rest of the trip was uneventful.

▲ ▲ ▲

Paul couldn't fall asleep again, startled as he was by his dream. His heart had stopped racing long ago, but his mind hadn't slowed down a bit. He didn't know what the dream meant, if anything at all—but if it did mean something, Paul knew he was destined to discover it.

The tram eventually came to a screeching halt when it arrived at Nautical. Seeing the name of the city lit up on the overhead display was somewhat of a triumph for Paul. He had finally made it. Now all he had to do was explore and put together the puzzle that had become askew. The obvious place for him to start would be the orphanage. It was located in Sawyer, a small town nearly 100 miles southwest of Nautical.

Paul exited the tram with thoughts of his journey on his mind. He grabbed his large, gray footlocker on the way out. The wheels hit the ground hard when he pulled it free from the luggage compartment. He imagined he could hear it moan from exhaustion.

Paul pulled it behind him as he crossed the tram terminal and walked out the front door. A large, flashing sign that read "Welcome to Nautical" greeted him and the other newcomers. Underneath it was a similar sign, only smaller, that read "Population: 1,274,490." Paul had no idea the city was so gigantic. Having grown up in Sawyer with a population of less than 10,000, Paul felt like a grain of sand walking onto a beach for the first time.

The late afternoon sun was shining brightly, but in the far west Paul could see the edge of rain clouds. Perhaps they were part of the storm he and Rapper had seen earlier. The weather forecast had predicted that a large front was sweeping across the country.

Nautical appeared to be a cheerful place. Street signs had small stars on them, similar to the ones on Paul's blanket. Hovercars—most of them soaring above the ground by about a foot—flew busily through the streets. Flashes of red, blue, black and white zipped from one end of the city to another. Pedestrians packed the sidewalks, wearing unusual combinations and outfits that were destined to be out of style in a matter of minutes. The hilly streets and pitted sidewalks made walking cumbersome, though no one seemed to notice.

Paul's stomach grumbled and he walked to a nearby hot dog vendor. The man had three sizes of hot dogs and 25 toppings, including "mystery meat sauce"—an addition Paul decided he could do without.

"Woof!"

"Hey, Spot," Paul greeted the hot dog vendor's Dalmatian with the first name that came to his mind. Paul ordered a medium-sized hot dog on a whole-wheat bun. The spotted dog barked again.

The vendor handed Paul a steaming hot dog with one hand and reached out for payment with the other. Paul slipped his hand in his back pants pocket, pulled out the payment and handed it to the man, who nodded. Paul slopped ketchup, mustard, relish and onions on his hot dog.

"Woof!"

"What are you barking at, girl?" Paul asked the Dalmatian.

"Mi' be your luggage," the vendor stated flatly, motioning down the hill with his thumb.

Paul looked down the hill. "My luggage? Why would he be barking at my—" Suddenly Paul's mouth dropped when he spied his footlocker rolling full-speed down the sharp incline.

"Aaahhhh!" Paul took off in an anxious run. He threw his hot dog down and the Dalmatian caught it before it even hit the ground. Paul charged after his runaway luggage, hoping someone would stop it. To his dismay, however, people parted in droves, like the Red Sea before Moses, and just watched as Paul rushed after it.

"Somebody stop that footlocker!" Paul shouted. The box hit a gash in the sidewalk and flipped into the air. It sailed freely for a few seconds and then thumped down again, back on its wheels, heading straight for a busy intersection.

Hovercars shot back and forth through the street, unaware of Paul's approaching square bullet.

"My clothes!" Paul shouted to no one in particular. The footlocker rolled with accelerating speed toward the intersection. Boom! It hit the curb and sailed onto the street pavement just as the light turned red, halting all vehicles in its path. The footlocker bolted across the street, rolled up a utility ramp and—with the force of speed behind it—began to make its ascent up the hill.

HONK-HONK! BEEP! "Get out of the way!!!"

Paul hit the intersection just as the light turned green again. He ran back to the curb and repeatedly hit the "WALK" button, hoping to halt traffic and get across to his runaway luggage quickly. Finally, the light turned red once more and the rushing traffic stopped. Paul ran across the street and then screamed when he saw his footlocker. It was coming straight toward him. At full speed.

Paul ran back across the street with the rolling luggage on his heels. His lungs were fighting for breath. Paul hopped up onto the curb and watched behind him as his luggage hit the curb a millisecond later. Impacting at full force, the massive box launched into the air and sailed over Paul's head.

Paul stepped back and watched as the huge foot-locker came tumbling down in slow motion. Paul braced himself on the sidewalk. With a loud THUD! the case hit the ground, wheels first, and Paul grabbed the handle with a tight fist. The wheels froze.

"Oooooohhhh," the square footlocker moaned. Paul jumped back. To his recollection, he had never heard a piece of luggage wail in pain. It began to roll again, but Paul quickly grabbed its handle and tossed it flat on its side. He knelt down beside it.

"Ouch!" it cried. Then it began to rumble on the pavement, like bubbles in a boiling pot of water. "I have had enough of this!" came a muffled shout.

The electronic clasps popped open with two beeps each—first the left, then the right. Paul scooted back when 10 tiny fingers with bright red fingernails peeked out of a crack in the middle and searched for the touch-key panel. When they found it, the fingers clumsily tapped in the correct combination and the top flopped open.

"Oh! Do I have one *splitting* headache!"

"Missy?!!!" Paul shouted, unable to believe his eyes. "No-no. Wait. This is just another nightmare. I'll wake up in a second."

"And to think I could have been relaxing in the sun on Calypso Island right now..."

"I don't believe this is happening." Paul slapped himself in the face. "Wake up. It's a dream."

Missy reached over and pulled a hair off the back of Paul's hand. He yelped.

"Good morning," she sang. "Oh, the things I go through for my friends..."

"Things you—Missy! I didn't *ask* you to come! You-you-you *stowed away* in my luggage?! Are you *crazy?* Do you know how *dangerous* that is?"

"Apparently *extremely* dangerous when it's *your* luggage," she said flatly. "Now help me out."

"I don't believe this." Paul grabbed Missy's hand and pulled her out of the footlocker. Suddenly, she doubled over and grabbed her calves.

"Cramps! I've got *cramps!* Ugh!!!" Missy looked up and realized for the first time that they were surrounded by a crowd of onlookers.

"What're you all looking at?" she addressed the crowd.

"Yeah," Paul added. "There's nothing unusual here except a stowaway popping out of a footlocker."

Missy flashed Paul a piercing look. Paul ignored it. Slowly, the crowd dispersed.

"I am not a stowaway," Missy countered, massaging her legs. "I'm an innovative traveler. Besides, a stowaway is someone who secretly goes on a trip without anyone knowing."

"So you're saying that someone else knows about this?"

"Commander Kellie."

"Commander Kellie knows you stowed away?"

"In a manner of speaking."

"In a manner of speaking..."

"She didn't know about it this morning, but she knows about it now. I left her a note."

"Oh, well, as long as you're being responsible." Paul rolled his eyes on the word "responsible."

"Hey, you're the one who needed help."

"I think *you're* the one who needs—" Paul's eyes dropped to the open footlocker. "Where are my clothes?"

Missy gave Paul a toothy smile. "There wasn't room. Sorry."

Paul reached down and picked up a small, circular, pink device from inside the footlocker. "And what is *this?*" he wondered. Missy twisted a lock of her blond hair around her index finger.

"My hair dryer."

"You had enough room for your hair dryer, but not for my clothes?!"

"Essentials, Paul! Think *essentials.* Don't worry. I made it a point to bring along your blanket since it's the only clue we have so far to finding your parents."

"Essentials? What am I supposed to *wear?* What are *you* supposed to wear?"

"Paul, my parents live here, remember? I have a whole wardrobe back at home."

Paul reached over, snapped the footlocker shut, locking in the blanket and hair dryer. He stood up. "Well, as long as you've thought this through." Missy looked down and spread out her hands at her side. Frustrated, Paul began to walk back up the street, dragging the footlocker behind him.

"I'm just trying to help," Missy said slowly and softly. Paul whipped around.

"Well, you're not."

Missy's eyes glassed over and her lips tightened. "I'm sorry," she whispered. "I can go back on the next tram. I didn't want to make things hard for you."

The sight of Missy tearing up caused a lump to form in Paul's throat. He let out a long, slow breath. "No, no...you're here now," he said, placing a hand on Missy's shoulder. "I'm sorry, too. It's just that—well, sometimes you pester me. You're acting like a little sister."

A tear crawled down Missy's cheek and dropped off her chin. She looked up and came eye-to-eye with Paul. "I thought that's what you wanted," she whispered.

Missy's house *wasn't* a house. It was a mansion. Set up on a grassy hill with a private drive and a security fence, Missy's house looked like something straight out of a fairy tale. The bushes were trimmed, the windows sparkled and the six white pillars around the porch were freshly painted and set in marble. On either side of the main walk to the house, a fountain shot glistening water heavenward.

Paul and Missy exited a bright yellow hovercar and Paul reached in his pocket to pay the driver.

"No need," the driver insisted, pushing Paul's money away. "Mr. Ashton is my boss." The cab lifted up and cruised away as Paul looked at Missy for an explanation. She shrugged.

"Daddy owns lots of stuff," she said, as if the statement explained everything.

Paul took a step forward and gasped when his foot tapped the sidewalk ahead of him. The entire walkway lit up in white brilliance in response to his touch. In the cool evening weather, the beauty of it all made Paul shudder.

"High-tech," Paul observed.

"With daddy, *everything* is high-tech," Missy countered. "C'mon, let's go!" Despite their confrontation only an hour ago, Missy was in elated spirits—especially happy to see her parents. Paul, on the other hand, felt slightly apprehensive. This is what he hadn't wanted: to be continually reminded that he didn't have a family, while everyone else did.

Missy ran up to the front door, but Paul took his time. When she reached the entrance, Missy signaled for Paul to hurry. He broke into a slow jog, which looked less enthusiastic than he had hoped. Just before he reached the door, it slid open and two faces beamed at Missy.

"Tootle!" the woman cried, reaching out and hugging Missy tightly. *"Tootle?"* Paul thought.

Missy leaned back from the hug and carefully kissed the woman once on each cheek as the woman did the same to Missy. Paul hoped he was blending into the pillar he stood beside—this was *too* embarrassing. Next, Missy hugged and kissed the man in the same fashion. Then she grabbed Paul's right arm and pulled him into the action.

"Mommy, Daddy, this is Paul Temp from Superkid Academy. He's on the Blue Squad, too."

"Pleased to meet you. You look like a fine young gentleman." Mr. Ashton offered a handshake and Paul accepted. Missy's dad was about 6 feet tall with white, receding hair and a clean-shaven face. A large nose sat comfortably below a pair of brown, penetrating eyes and two bushy, white eyebrows. He wore a green sweater, khaki pants and loafers.

"My pleasure," Mrs. Ashton offered her hand also. At first, Paul reached out to shake it, but he caught Missy—out of the corner of his eye—puckering her lips. Paul got the clue. He kissed the back of Mrs. Ashton's hand and smiled nicely. Mrs. Ashton looked as though she'd never aged over 29. Beautifully styled long, blond hair curled around her soft facial features, which were accented by her blue eyes. If she were any younger, she could probably have passed for Missy's sister. She wore a bright green dress with a pearl necklace linked around her collar. The outfit was complete with a pair of matching, bright green flats. Both of Missy's parents appeared lean and in good health.

"My daddy's name is Gregg and my mommy's name is Lois. But you can call them Mr. and Mrs. Ashton," Missy stated politely. Paul chuckled. He had planned to give them that respect anyway.

▲   ▲   ▲

Roasted chicken basted in an herb sauce, new potatoes, baby peas, Waldorf salad and carrot cake for dessert. It wasn't an unpleasant first night in Nautical. Paul was beginning to think having Missy along wasn't such a bad deal after all. In the few hours he'd spent with the Ashtons so far, he'd really warmed up to them. They were polite, loving and giving. Paul wasn't sure what he had expected Missy's parents to be like, but this wasn't it. This was much better. Meeting them also helped him to understand Missy more.

At one time, he thought Missy was overbearing, but now he understood that her determination and black-and-white attitude came from her dad's side of the family. In the course of conversation, Paul found out he was a sharp businessman who believed in doing what was right no matter what the cost. In the end, these qualities made him quite successful.

It was also tempting (at times) to think Missy was vain because of the vast amount of time she spent in front of the mirror. But the truth was, Missy grew up considering what Paul called "a formal appearance" to be everyday normality. Paul realized that maybe it wasn't Missy who was so different. Maybe it was him. Having grown up in a poor orphanage, he never saw such things on a normal basis.

Paul took a few gulps of milk. It tasted great after the long day on the tram.

"So how do you like our little town?" Mrs. Ashton inquired. She sat opposite Mr. Ashton, and Missy sat across from Paul.

"It's really big compared to what I'm used to," Paul replied. "I like it though."

"How did you get here?" Mrs. Ashton wondered after a bite of chicken. "Did you fly?"

"No, we came by tram." Paul looked at Missy. "Though I had a little luggage trouble when I arrived."

Missy's foot caught Paul in the shin. He nearly dropped his milk glass.

"So what's your business down here?" Mr. Ashton asked. He shoved a forkful of new potatoes into his mouth.

Paul wiped his lips with his napkin. His stomach was full and satisfied. He carefully set the napkin back down in his lap and then replied to Mr. Ashton's question.

"I'm looking for my parents."

Mrs. Ashton stopped chewing. "Your parents are lost?"

"Well, not exactly. I'm the one who's lost. I'm an orphan."

"I see." Mr. Ashton nodded. The room fell quiet. Then, Mr. Ashton's wife leaned in and whispered across the table, as if no one else were in the room.

"Gregg, you can't just drop the conversation there. He's *begging* for help!"

Now I know where Missy gets her feistiness, Paul reasoned silently.

Mr. Ashton gazed at his wife with a questioning look on his face. Then he turned to Paul.

"You need any help, boy? My resources are at your disposal."

Paul shook his head. "No, Missy thought I needed help, too. But, really, I'm fine."

"You've got a good head on your shoulders, Tootle," Mrs. Ashton complimented Missy. Missy squeezed her eyes tightly and smiled.

"I'm going to the orphanage tomorrow," Paul added. "I'm hoping they can give me the leads I need. It's in Sawyer—you know where that is?"

Mr. Ashton patted his lips and chin with his napkin and cleared his throat. "Why, yes, I think I do. It is a dusty, little town, isn't it?"

"Yeah, it is," Paul snickered. If there was one thing he remembered from his years in Sawyer, it was that the whole place was windy and dusty. A small town of miners, Sawyer wasn't the kind of town most people noticed. There were no high-speed tram services, no malls and no suburbs.

"But what brings you into Nautical, Paul? Surely there are towns closer to Sawyer with tramports." Mrs. Ashton appeared genuinely concerned.

"Well," Paul admitted, pushing aside his dinner plate, "maybe you can help me with that. I actually have a clue that my parents are from Nautical. I have a blanket in my footlocker—it's blue and white striped with—"

"—gold lettering on it," Mr. Ashton interrupted.

"Yes!" Paul shouted, jumping up from his chair. His eyes were wide with excitement. "Do you know who makes them? Where they're sold? It might help me narrow down my search!"

"Paul, I think you'd better sit down." Gregg Ashton's face was grim. "I don't have very good news for you." Paul felt his heart sink inside his chest. He'd only barely begun his search and not much was going right. Slowly,

Paul sat down. He didn't bother to pull himself up to the elegantly clothed table. Missy's mother began explaining.

"The blanket you're describing was made by Nautical Fabrics."

A clue! Paul thought. "So what's the bad news?"

Mr. Ashton's brown eyes peered at Paul beneath his bushy, white eyebrows. "Up until about nine years ago, Nautical Fabrics gave every newborn in every hospital a copy of the exact blanket you received. Missy even received one when we brought her home from the hospital."

"I did?" Missy questioned.

"Yes," her mother replied, whispering loudly on the side. "You had it until you were 2, Tootle. Then you started complaining that the blue stripes clashed with your designer diapers. I got rid of it right away."

Missy nodded. Her father continued.

"Paul, the point is that there are hundreds of thousands of those blankets out there. If a child was born in Nautical, he received one. It was a gift from the city."

Paul took it all in. The blanket had no hidden, special meaning. It was just a blanket—a blanket *everyone* had. He was back at square one.

"Wait!" Paul noted. "But it still proves I was born in Nautical. I didn't even know *that* before."

"That's true," Missy encouraged. "And maybe if we can find the factory that gave away those blankets, you can talk to someone. Maybe there are records or something."

"That might be hard, too, Tootle," Missy's father blatantly said. "There's a reason they stopped giving away blankets nine years ago."

Paul's eyebrows lifted, wrinkling his forehead. Gregg Ashton continued.

"Nine years ago, they were abruptly put out of business when the government found out some of their dealings were highly illegal. Apparently, there was more going on than just selling fabric. Actually, it was their closing that made Ashton Clothiers number one in Nautical...and it gave us the financial ability to launch nationwide."

A realization hit Paul. "You mean you're the *owner* of Ashton Clothiers?" Ashton Clothiers was the country's largest maker of cloth products—from underclothes to heavy jackets, from tablecloths to bedroom ensembles. As long as Paul could remember, he had been wearing clothes by Ashton Clothiers. They were durable, fairly priced and quality guaranteed.

"The one and only," Mr. Ashton admitted. "But that won't help you here. Nautical Fabrics doesn't exist anymore. That's a dead end."

Paul nodded. There was so much to think about.

"There's still your orphanage in...where was it...Sawyer? Maybe you'll find something there."

"Maybe," Paul mumbled. He huffed, "Maybe."

"We'll go there tomorrow," Missy encouraged, reaching across the table with a helping hand. She grabbed Paul's forearm, which he had propped on the table's edge. "I'll help you."

A long silence prevailed. Then, Mrs. Ashton leaned over to Missy and whispered loudly, "You're such a good encourager, Tootle." Then she turned to Paul. "You know, Missy has always been an encouragement to us. Even when she was a baby, she used to smile all the time."

Paul smiled at Missy. Missy smiled back.

"In fact," Missy's mother continued, "that's why we call her 'Tootle.'"

"Mother..." Missy was raising an eyebrow.

"What, Honey? I wasn't going to tell him you smiled because you passed—"

"*MOTHER!!*" Missy's hand snapped away from Paul and both arms clung to her sides. Her mouth dropped and her face washed bright red as she covered it with her hands. "Oh! I am *so* embarrassed!"

"What?"

"Oh, I am *sooooo embaaaaarrassed!*"

"What? Did I say something wrong?"

Paul felt embarrassed too—more for Missy than himself. On the good side, the distraction created the perfect opportunity for an exit on a tiring day. Mr. Ashton must have been looking to depart, too, for he was quick to stand up and address Paul.

"Why don't I show you a guest room?" he asked. "Do you have a preference?"

"Preference?"

"Yes, we have six," Mr. Ashton responded.

"You have *six* guest rooms?" Paul was astounded. *This isn't a house, it's a hotel.* Paul looked at Missy and her mother still debating in hushed tones. "I'll take the nearest one," Paul decided, standing up.

Gregg Ashton retreated from the dining room with Paul to show him the way to his temporary quarters. As they walked out, Paul turned his head to nod good night to Missy. She wasn't looking, though. Her head was aimed skyward.

"Oh, I am *sooo* embarrassed!"

▲   ▲   ▲

"You know, Paul, I was an orphan, too."

Paul nearly stumbled up the stairs as he walked with Mr. Ashton. *"You* were an orphan? Wow."

"What's so amazing about that?"

"Well, you're just so successful, sir. I mean...wow."

"You need to change your thinking, boy," Mr. Ashton said as they trekked down a long hall.

Paul pondered Mr. Ashton's words but didn't quite understand. He had to ask, "Are you saying you don't think I should be looking for my family?"

Mr. Ashton stopped walking. Paul stopped too.

"What I'm saying, son, is that just because you're an orphan doesn't mean you're destined to be less than anyone else. You're not 'lost.' You've been adopted into God's family now and He sees you as very special."

"You know, a friend of mine said almost the same thing last night—about being adopted into God's family. I'm not sure I understand it all yet, but it has something to do with the covenant God made with us."

Mr. Ashton began walking again and Paul followed.

"Yes sir," Mr. Ashton said winking at Paul, "a covenant is a powerful thing. Abraham had a covenant with God. David and Jonathan had a covenant with each other. Even I once had a covenant like that with a friend."

"You did?"

"Mmmm-hmmm. Many years ago, he and his wife and son were killed in a tram wreck, but as far as I'm concerned, our covenant still exists. He was my best friend. And the covenant between us—the loyalty we shared—it was like we were part of each other's family. It helped me to see the covenant God has with us. I'm telling you the truth, son. Realize it or not, you're not an orphan anymore. You've been adopted into God's family."

"I just want to know who they are, *where* they are... and if they love me."

Mr. Ashton stopped walking again and turned to Paul.

"This is where we say good night."

"Why?" Paul wondered. "Did I say something wrong?"

"No," Mr. Ashton responded with a smile. He tapped on a touchpad and a door slid open. "This is your room."

If there was such a thing as a perfect night's sleep, Paul had it. Paul woke up early, revived and once again encouraged. Lying in bed, he pondered the day ahead, anticipating what he might discover at the orphanage. Before rising, Paul prayed for a while in the spirit, then he softly sang a worship song he had written only weeks before...

> *Early in the morning*
> *I'll lift up songs of praise*
> *Songs of thanks and honor*
> *Songs of love ablaze*
>
> *And late, late in the evening*
> *I'll worship Your Holy Name*
> *For You give me the victory*
> *You're forever the same*
>
> *Without shame, I'll worship You, my Lord*
> *Lifting up Your Name, I'll shout Your praises*
> *I will proclaim Your Word of victory*
> *And I will tell of all You've done for me*

Paul pushed back the covers and jumped out of bed. He stumbled toward the bathroom, but stopped midway. Where he'd left his dirty clothes the night before, there were now three bright, brand-new outfits—each one with a set of pants, underclothes and a rugby. Inside tags proclaimed "Ashton Clothiers" and everything was exactly his size. A small, folded note sat beside the stack of outfits. Paul popped it open with his fingers. Inside, written in what looked like Missy's mother's handwriting, were the words:

> Paul,
>
> We have set ourselves in agreement with you.
>
> Remember Matt. 18:19-20—
>
> Jesus said, "I tell you that if two of you on earth agree about anything you ask for, it will be done for you by my Father in heaven.
>
> For where two or three come together in my name, there am I with them."
>
> We pray you'll find the truth you're looking for.
>
> The Ashtons

Smiling and relieved to have some fresh clothes, Paul set down the note. He chose an ensemble that consisted of a pair of black jeans and a blue, green and off-white patched rugby. After showering, he dressed. Everything fit perfectly. As he pulled the rugby over his head, his thoughts reflected back to Rapper's story about how, to signify an exchanging of authority in a covenant, two people would exchange clothes. It hit Paul as he adjusted his shirt that, as long as he was with the Ashtons, he had the authority of the family behind him. "If you need any help," Mr. Ashton had said, "my resources are at your disposal." And even the note proved that they were in agreement with Paul.

Still, Paul was a bit puzzled. He hadn't done anything to deserve their help. But they were offering it. Paul pondered this as he finished getting ready.

Set for the day, Paul left his room and wandered down the hall. Plush, sandy-colored carpeting lined the walkway. He passed a library, an office and several closed doors. Pictures lined the walls, interrupted only by the entrances to the rooms. Paul walked slowly, taking in snapshots of Missy's parents at their wedding. Mr. Ashton looked years younger with a full head of brown hair and a wrinkleless face. Mrs. Ashton looked remarkably the same as she did when Paul saw her the evening before. In some pictures, Paul first thought he was looking at Missy—and then realized it was her mother as a teenager.

Grandfathers, grandmothers, aunts, uncles, cousins and friends smiled at Paul as he walked by. Paul could almost hear the laughter and feel the love. It made him more determined than ever to find his parents. He had to find his family.

Finally, Paul reached the room that Gregg Ashton said was his daughter's, and he knocked on the door.

"Tootle! Are you in there?" he taunted.

The door slid open and Missy's head popped out. Paul yelped. Her hair was straight and wet, peeking out from underneath a towel wrapped around her head like a turban. One eye had black lining on it and there was even a pimple on her chin. Paul had *never* seen a zit on Missy. Not even the past year when the Blue Squad was stranded for an entire weekend on a hot, sweltering island without being able to bathe or eat much. Even then, Missy never got a blemish. This was new ground.

"You can't call me 'Tootle!'" she shouted as an order. "Only Mommy and Daddy can."

"Good morning to you, too," Paul said with a laugh. "Hey, where is everybody?"

"Daddy's at work...and I think Mommy said she had to go to a charity auction. You're welcome to help yourself to breakfast." Her hair was dripping on the floor.

"I'll wait for you."

"Oh, I already ate. I prefer to get food out of the way before I apply my makeup. But help yourself—you remember where the kitchen is."

"Yup. How much longer do you think you'll be?"

"Probably just a few minutes."

"Five? Ten?"

"Sixty."

"You want an hour?! Missy, I wanna get started!"

"I'll hurry," she promised. "Now go get some food. You're cranky."

▲   ▲   ▲

Paul poured himself a bowl of *Wheatsie Eatsies* cereal and, as he crunched, he read from a leather-bound Bible he found on the kitchen counter. He had opened it to Galatians 3.

"All who believe today are blessed just as Abraham was blessed. Christ took away that curse. He changed places with us and put himself under that curse."

Paul thought back to his dream and how the figure changed places with him...

"It is written in the scriptures, 'Everyone whose body is displayed on a tree is cursed.' Christ did this so that God's blessing promised to Abraham might come..."

What is the blessing God promised to Abraham? the Holy Spirit questioned Paul in his spirit. *What is the curse Jesus took away on the cross?*

Paul leaned back and rubbed his eyes. He knew God was showing him something. Something he needed to know. Paul thought back to Rapper's conversation with him and Alex two nights before. Rapper had talked about God's covenant with Abram.

"That's it!" Paul said aloud to himself. "This is talking about the covenant God made with Abram, whose name changed to Abraham. So, where in the Bible does it talk about this covenant and the blessings God promised to Abraham?"

Deuteronomy 28. The answer leapt in his spirit. Paul pushed aside his breakfast bowl and flipped the pages of the Bible. He found the passage.

"You will be blessed in the city and blessed in the country. The fruit of your womb will be blessed...your basket and your kneading trough will be blessed. You will be blessed when you come in and blessed when you go out. The Lord will grant that the enemies who rise up against you will be defeated before you...The Lord your God will send a blessing on your barns....The Lord will bless you in the land he is giving you. The Lord will establish you as his holy people...The Lord will open up the heavens, the storehouse of his bounty...He will bless all the work of your hands."

Whoa! Paul thought. *God promised all that to Abraham?*

Those promises are for you, too, the Holy Spirit affirmed, *if you'll believe.*

Paul flipped the Bible back to Galatians 3. It said, "Jesus died so that we could have the Spirit that God promised and receive this promise by believing."

I will believe, Paul decided. *I need these blessings now if I'm to find the answer about my parents.*

Then Paul read the list of curses in Deuteronomy 28. They included trouble on every corner, confusion and punishment. Terrible diseases, sickness, starvation and abuse. Reading all the curses excited Paul, too. *These are all the curses Jesus took away on the cross! I don't have to live with them! But...why? Why did Jesus die for us? Why would He go through all that?*

Paul's thoughts were interrupted when the ComPhone rang. He walked over to it and looked at the digital identi-fication readout. It was a call from Superkid Academy. Paul pushed the answer button and Rapper's face popped up on a tiny monitor.

"Hey, Paul!"

"Rapper! Hey, bud! How'd you know I was here?"

"Commander Kellie got Missy's note," Rapper explained. "She's not real happy about it either. I think she's going to make Missy pay the tram company full fare for her ride and then she's going to assign her extra duties when she gets back. I don't envy Missy's position."

"She shouldn't have done it," Paul agreed. "But I shouldn't have told her not to come, either. I'm actually starting to appreciate her being here."

"Find out anything yet?"

"Nope—but we're going to my old orphanage this morning, as soon as Missy's done getting ready."

"So you mean you're going to your old orphanage this *afternoon...*"

"Yeah," Paul laughed. "Hey, aren't you supposed to be on Calypso Island?"

"The weather has been too rough. But it's clearing up—heading your way, I believe. Anyway, I think we'll head out early this afternoon. Now that Missy joined you, it'll be just me and Val."

"Well, you two have fun. Don't eat too much wild boar."

Rapper licked his lips. "I get *your* portion! Well, just wanted to make sure the two of you were all right. We're standing in agreement with you!"

"Thanks. Paul out."

"Rapper out."

Paul pushed a button marked "disconnect" and Rapper's face fizzled away.

Paul looked at his watch. Forty-five minutes had ticked away. He put away the food and the Bible and retired to the living room. It was filled with colorful flower bouquets and little bowls of mints. On the right side of the room, a sofa faced out, angled toward two Victorian chairs on either side of a fireplace. Paul walked over to the fireplace mantle and looked at the collection of pictures on top—all in different types of frames.

This time the pictures were almost all of Missy. Missy as a baby in the arms of friends, crying as a teddy bear is held above her. Missy as a baby again, this time slumped up on a yellow, carpeted ramp. Missy walking down a lighted aisle with a rose, a crown and a banner that proclaimed "Little Miss Nautical." Missy in pony-tails, riding her first, shiny, red air-scooter. Missy eating a big bowl of cookie batter—her face covered with chocolate chips. Missy making faces at the camera with her friends. And finally, Missy standing stately in her Superkid uniform. Missy everywhere!

"Hey!" Missy shouted, entering the room. "I'm ready."

Missy was dressed in black jeans, too, topped off with a violet, velvet blouse. She wore black ankle boots and a thin, dark belt. A gold necklace was linked around her neck. Her blond hair was curly and perfect, and her makeup accented her high cheekbones. The pimple was remarkably nonexistent and her teeth shone bright white. She was beautiful.

"Like your shrine," Paul said offhandedly, angling his thumb toward the mantle.

"Thank you." Missy smiled sweetly. "Let's go. I thought we could take some high-powered air-scooters if you'd like."

"You have high-powered ones?"

"We've got GRXs. My dad—"

"—owns the company," they both said in unison. Missy laughed. "Well, he does."

A Real Treasure

Atop two top-of-the-line GRX air-scooters, Paul and Missy shot down the road at high speed. The air-scooters were built to look and feel like vintage motorcycles, but they were "souped up" (in Paul's words) to run at faster speeds and glide on air. Each sailed well above the ground, with the rider on top, leaning far forward to reinforce the aerodynamic design.

The vehicles, like most others Paul was used to, were virtually silent, with the exception of a soft *whoosh* of air that ran through the engine. The ride to Sawyer took an hour, even at full speed, and they were both glad to stretch when they arrived. Paul led Missy through the familiar, dusty town to the far edge where his orphanage residence was located. Dark clouds were beginning to move in from the west. Paul hoped the clouds would hold their moisture.

When they came to a stop and parked their air-scooters outside of the little, gray house, Missy blinked noticeably. "Looks poor."

"It *is* poor," Paul confirmed. "But this is where I grew up. If anyone has a clue about my mom or dad, it'll be found here."

Missy wiped her cheek. A thin film of dust transferred to the back of her hand. "Great. It's dusty, too."

"Paul Temp!" The gray-haired head of a woman popped out of the upper story of the two-level dwelling. "Is that you?!"

"It's me!" Paul shouted up. The woman promptly disappeared from the window. Paul could hear her bounding down the stairs inside. Missy raised her eyebrows in question. The front door slid open and the woman, 5 ½ feet tall with a wide frame and rosy cheeks, hopped down the porch stairs to meet them.

"Oh, my goodness, little one—you're not so little anymore!"

Paul grabbed the woman and gave her a hug. Then she took a step back and spied Missy from head to toe.

"And who is this little angel?" she asked, sounding more nosey than curious.

"Gran, meet Missy Ashton, a good friend of mine from the Academy—Missy Ashton, Gran." They shook hands politely. The old woman invited them inside. Paul looked around, but didn't see any familiar faces. Children from the ages of 2 to 10 danced around the house. Some were playing with blocks, some were drawing and some were running around. Paul noticed a group playing freeze tag out the back window.

Paul and Missy accepted a couple seats in Gran's large kitchen. She brought each of them a tall glass of homemade cherry lemonade.

"This is wonderful!" Missy complimented, after a swallow.

"A cold drink after a long journey. Now, Paul, you weren't riding one of those air-scooters, were you?"

Paul nodded. "I was, but don't worry. I was driving safely and responsibly."

"You are such a good boy," Gran flattered Paul.

"He is such a good *sweet-talker*," Missy corrected, jabbing Paul in the ribs with her elbow. Paul laughed. Paul told Missy about Gran—how she'd taken care of him growing up, along with so many other kids. And Gran doted on Paul, telling Missy how she'd been a caretaker for 20 years, brought up more than 60 children, yet Paul was her favorite of all. Paul assured Missy that she said that about every one of the kids. The two shared stories they recollected and laughed. Missy laughed, too, but looked a little sad. Paul knew exactly what was going through her mind. He knew she was excited to hear all about Paul's early life and his good memories...but it saddened her that in the crowd of children, he was still alone. She knew his heart. She knew that more than anything else, he wanted a family...and as loving as Gran and the other kids were, it wasn't the same to him.

"Well," Gran finally said after their glasses were all bone-dry, "Paul, if I know you, there's more to your visit than just remembering old stories."

"It's true," Paul acknowledged. "Gran, can you tell me about my parents? I'm trying to find them. I found a clue last week that led me to believe they lived in Nautical. But I'm hoping you can help me narrow down my search."

"Paul, you know I normally don't give out that kind of information. Most of our kids are from abusive families. They were forced to come here because their parents didn't care for them properly." Her eyes sank at the thought of someone hurting a child.

"So my parents didn't love me?"

"I have a feeling your mother loved you very much," Gran corrected him.

"So you *can* tell me something?"

"Well...I suppose I can...but only because I believe your mother was a good woman." Paul and Missy both leaned forward.

"I can remember it as though it was only yesterday," Gran lamented. "The night was cool and my window was open. Suddenly, I was jolted awake with a notion to pray. And I did—for the rest of the night. The next morning, as I was making breakfast, I heard a cry on the porch. Well, at first I thought one of my little ones was up early and had hurt themselves. So I ran to the front door. When I opened it, there you were—wrapped tight in a blue, white and gold blanket, clutching a stuffed animal and crying like the wind. I picked you up and there were bruises all over your body. I'd seen bruises like that before. You can imagine how my heart broke.

"The fog was so thick that morning I could barely see. But on the western horizon I saw a woman, traveling alone. A moment later, she disappeared into the fog. I believe to this day it was your mother. I don't know anything about your father, Paul, but I know your mother saved you from a bad situation by doing the best thing she knew. She entrusted your care—your life—to the orphanage.

"I had our local doctor come over that day and he said it looked like you'd even been unconscious for a while before you were delivered here." Gran stopped talking for a moment and bit her lip. Then she continued. "So, anyway, I told him how your mother left you here to save you. He told me you were blessed to be brought here when you were. Another day in a home like that and you might not have...well, so I took you in and called you 'Paul Temp.'"

The woman grabbed Missy's wrist with her hand and whispered, "'Paul' was the name of my late husband whom I loved so much...And 'Temp,' well, that's just the last name we always gave to kids whose parents we hoped to find—it's short for 'temporary.' But for Paul...well...I guess it became permanent."

"Paul Temp," Missy repeated softly.

Paul felt his hope sink into his stomach. Fourteen years had passed and his last name was proof he was abandoned. And worse, his mother was last seen traveling west...away from Nautical.

"She never returned...never called?"

Gran shook her head. "I had hoped she would one day, but no. I'm sorry."

Missy slowly brushed a lock of her blond hair behind her ear. "Paul, maybe it's time to accept that—"

"I have the blanket she left with me, but do you have the stuffed animal?" Paul interrupted Missy. Gran's bottom lip protruded. Then her face lit up. She got up and walked out of the room. "Well, c'mon..." she ushered. Missy didn't move.

"You never know," Paul coaxed. Missy nodded and rose. They followed Gran up the rickety, gray stairs to her bedroom. It was a simple room, reflecting Gran herself, with a single bed, a night stand and alarm clock, a lamp and a dresser. A few snapshots were stuck into the frame of a mirror above her dresser. As Gran opened her closet, Paul looked them over. Cute, blank faces stared back, each telling a story only a storyteller like Gran would remember.

"Check it out, here's me!" Paul said, picking up a photo of a little boy with a round face sticking his tongue out at the camera.

Missy touched it on the corner. "You were a little rebel, weren't you?"

"Naw," Paul shook his head, smiling.

Gran chuckled as she exited the closet with a brown box, folded into itself on the top. "Yes, he was. Ages 7 to

9 were Paul's 'Where-can-I-find-trouble?' years. And let me tell you, Missy, he did. Aged me 10 years, I think."

Missy giggled.

"Well, I didn't cause all that trouble myself," Paul defended, sticking the photo back into the mirror frame. "You remember Shea Brown? She was a little rebel, too."

"Sure, try to pass it off on someone else, Paul," Missy jabbed. "And a girl, no less."

"Well, I—"

"Mmmm-hmmm."

"But, I—aw, never mind."

Missy giggled again.

Gran popped open the top of the box. Dust launched into the air. Missy waved her hand. "That stuffed animal of yours would have been thrown in the toy box and left to compete with the dinosaurs, birds and elephants for space," Gran said, getting back to the subject at hand. "But I found out it was a collectible made by a man in town. So, I kept it for you and then forgot about it until now."

Gran pulled a small teddy bear from the box. It looked as though it had been played with one too many times. An eye was missing, the fur was matted and a tiny piece of candy cane was stuck on its sewn-up belly.

"Now *there's* a treasure," Missy remarked.

"May I have it?" Paul asked. Gran nodded. Missy gave Paul a double take. "May I talk to you for a moment?" Missy asked Paul, pulling him off to the side. "Paul," she whispered, "I don't know how to say this politely, but...well..." Missy judged every word before speaking. "That bear...it kinda, uh...*smells*...and, uh...looks...*gross.* I know it may have sentimental value...but let me buy you a new one. 'K?" Missy looked hopeful, but Paul didn't budge.

"Other than my blanket, this is the only link I have to my past. I don't want to lose it."

Missy scrunched up her face. "OK, but if you find cooties crawling in your bed at night, don't say I didn't warn you."

"Believe it or not, this *really* is a special find," Gran offered. "As I said, a man in Nautical has been making this bear for many years. He's at a shop on Seventh and...uh...Ryan Street, I believe. You could get a new one, but now that they're considered collector's items, they've become rather expensive."

"Hey, what's this?" Paul looked down at the bear to see where Missy was pointing. On a frayed tag, written in permanent marker were the words, "WINNER 25."

"Do you think it means something?" Missy wondered.

"Well, we're about to find out," Paul confirmed. "Let's go back to Nautical and pay a visit to Seventh and Ryan!"

Crack-BOOM! Lightning lit up the sky as thunder rolled in, sounding like an avalanche. Large raindrops smacked the window of the little shop on the corner of Seventh and Ryan. Though located within a section of Nautical that wasn't as bustling as it once had been, the shop appeared to be doing surprisingly well.

"Fiffer's Crafts and Collectibles" was a dainty shop filled with craft supplies, homemade gifts and various collectibles—from hand-painted sculptures to crystal figurines. The walls were lined with display cases and shelves, each containing something different, depending on each customer's interest. A row of unique bears, each representing a different occupation, filled the small, solitary front window. One was a fisherman, one was a cowboy, one was a doctor. Paul imagined it would take him half a day to count all the different lifestyles represented.

When they entered, an electronic bell sounded at the door and a thin, old man looked up. He was standing near some shelves packed with painting supplies and wiping down the floor with a mop. He wore a simple, white dress shirt, brown slacks and a thin, brown tie.

"Hey, kids," he greeted Paul and Missy. "I'm Mr. Fifopolis. Just call me 'Fiffer'—all my friends do.

Interested in a craft today? Or maybe buying a special gift for a loved one?"

Paul approached the man and handed his worn, stuffed bear to him. Fiffer winced, apparently appalled at the condition of the dirty, matted animal.

"You need a new one?" he asked.

"How'd you guess?" Missy muttered on the side.

"Actually, no," Paul answered, shooting a sideways glance at Missy. "I'm wondering if you can tell me about *this* one."

Fiffer set his mop in a pail of murky water and gave the stuffed animal his full attention.

"It's definitely one of mine. Looks old. I dunno. Maybe I could repair it. Give it new eyes, resew its belly, clean its fur..."

"I'd appreciate that. Consider it a deal. But what I really want to know is, can you tell me who you sold it to?" Paul wondered. Fiffer shook his head.

"Hmmm...can't help you there. I've sold nearly 20,000 of these bears. They've been my business. In fact, I just bought some land across the street to expand on. I'm so excited. So you can see why the chance of me knowing who bought this bear is about as good as chocolate milk comin' out of a cow."

Paul flipped the bear over in the old man's hands and stretched out the tag.

"Well, does this mean anything to you?"

Fiffer pulled his glasses down to the end of his nose and peered closely at the tag.

"Now, would you look at that...'Winner 25.' Boy, today's your day."

Paul's eyes opened wide. "You mean you know who you sold it to?"

Fiffer nodded. "Let's just say I owe you some chocolate milk. Truth is, I didn't sell this bear to anybody. Someone won it. And that someone should be in my records."

"Really?!" Missy shouted.

"Yes, ma'am. This is one of the first 25 bears I made. Good golly. That was 15 years ago. I gave my first 25 away in a contest to attract people to my business. I wrote down the names of every one of those winners, because I wanted to send them special mailings for my shop. Yes siree, I should have the name."

"Well, who is it?!" Missy cried.

"I have to know!" Paul insisted. The gentleman nodded and raised his finger, indicating that he wanted the Superkids to wait a moment. He walked into a back room and returned a few seconds later with a thick, three-ring binder. He walked behind his front counter and set it down between himself and the two Superkids. Paul saw the word "Ledger" typed on the front—it was a book for keeping track of money and other important information. Carefully, the store owner flipped it open. He searched up and down a few pages until he finally found what he was looking for. The page was titled "Lil'

Bear Winners" and it was full of penciled-in names. He unhooked the binder and pulled the page out, then re-snapped the binder shut. Setting the page down on the counter, he began to read.

"Winner number one, Raymond Woodall," he read. "Winner number two, Vicki Gordon. Winner number three, LeAnne Bonner. Winner number four—"

"Excuse me, sir," Paul interrupted. "Would you mind just going down to number 25?"

"Huh? Oh, right. Let's see." His finger slid down the page one number at a time. Paul clenched his fists. Missy rolled her eyes.

"Oh!" Fiffer exclaimed. "This page ends with number 20. Must be on the back." Paul almost reached over and grabbed the page. He knew Missy was thinking the same thing because she took a bold step toward the counter.

Fiffer began to turn over the page.

Beep! The bell sounded at the door, and in burst a man with a scraggly beard and hair to match. The rain had soaked his dark clothes, and Paul could smell the liquor on him as soon as he entered. The man scowled and threw his arm out in front of him. From within his fist, a switchblade shot out into the air.

"Nobody move 'cept for you, ol' man!" the criminal shouted. "Gimme all you's money!"

Fiffer slapped the paper down on the counter, front side up, and popped open his register. Paul couldn't believe the timing of the situation. The devil was working double time to keep Paul from finding his mother!

"Where do I put it?" Fiffer asked, holding a clump of cash. The thief drew close and pointed to a sack behind the register. "In 'ere," he indicated. Missy snarled at the thief. He turned and looked at her. His rotting teeth were clenched tight.

"Thassa pretty neckless you got," he hissed. Then, in one swift motion, he jerked it off Missy's neck.

"Ugh! Hey!" she cried. The thief placed a greasy hand under Missy's chin.

"You's a pretty one, ain'cha..."

That was all Paul could take. With a holy anger burning within, he lashed out with a clenched fist.

CRACK! Paul's fist smashed hard into the criminal's jaw. Missy jumped back as the criminal fumbled and reeled, surprised at the attack. The thief roared in anger and lurched forward. He came straight at Paul with his switchblade out. Paul moved sideways to avoid the attack, but the blade caught his left hand and sliced it on the palm. Paul cried out in pain. Suddenly, as he looked up, he saw Fiffer coming at the thief with a baseball bat.

Then it happened.

Lightning flashed.

Thunder roared.

The lights went out.

Paul heard a crash, a boom and felt a gust of cool air. Suddenly, backup lights flipped on, illuminating the darkness. The thief was gone and the shop's door was sliding shut. An electronic beep sounded.

Fiffer was breathing heavily, regaining his composure. He had broken his bat on a chair, which was now smashed. Missy ran over to Paul and looked at his hand.

"Oh!" she whimpered. Fiffer pointed to a door off to the side.

"There's a first-aid kit in there," he promised. Missy returned with the kit and confidently applied some soothing cream and a bandage to Paul's wound. It wasn't deep, but it was long. Paul silently thanked the Lord he hadn't caught the full force of the thief's knife thrust, or things could have been much worse. Missy finally finished wrapping Paul's hand when it hit him: the paper.

Paul jumped up and ran to the counter. It was gone. The money was still there, but the paper was gone!

"Where is it?!" Paul shouted. "Where's the paper?! I need that paper!"

Missy and Paul searched all around the counter—front and back, hoping to find it. Suddenly, Fiffer spoke up.

"I found it!" he hollered. Paul and Missy whipped around. Fiffer reached down and lifted it up, out of the murky, mop water. It was soaked and dripped on the floor. Paul couldn't believe it. The wind coming through the front door must have caught it. He ran over and gently took it out of Fiffer's hands. The man sighed. As Paul held it, the weight of the water pulled it to shreds from his hands. He tried to read it, but it was no use. The faded, penciled writing had worn away into a watery grave.

"I don't know what that paper meant to you," Fiffer said, "but I can tell by the look on your face, it was important. I'm sorry, son."

Fiffer squeezed Paul's shoulder, then retreated to report the robbery to the police. When he left the room, Paul leaned forward and put his hands on his legs. Missy joined him on the floor. She reached over and gave him a sideways hug.

"It'll be all right," she offered.

"None of this has been an accident," Paul began. "The devil is doing all he can do to keep me from finding my mother. I can totally see it. He knows that if I find my family, I'll have a strong, spiritual force on my side. When a family joins together in agreement about something, Satan doesn't stand a chance. He's trying to keep me from the truth."

"I'm sorry, Paul. I know this hurts. I understand."

"Why do people keep saying that!" Paul shouted, thumping the ground with his good hand. "No, you don't *understand!* I have lost my *family.* I've *lost* them! And there's *nothing* I can do about that! Have *you* ever lost your family? *No!* You don't understand."

"Yes I do!" Missy's sudden outburst shocked Paul. She pointed a finger in his face. "I *do* understand. Satan

stole a part of my family, too—and there was nothing I could do about it!" Missy turned her face away from Paul. Paul reached out and touched her shoulder. It was tense.

"Missy, what happened?"

"Nothing. Forget it."

"Missy...you can tell me."

Missy looked forward, not at Paul, but over his shoulder.

"I was supposed to have a brother," she finally whispered. Paul listened without saying a word. "I was supposed to have an older brother. See, years ago, my daddy's best friend and his family were killed."

Paul nodded and said softly, "Yeah, your dad mentioned that in passing last night. Said he had a covenant with him." This time Missy nodded.

"Well, what he probably didn't tell you was that he was with them when it happened. And someone else was with them, too. My older brother, Scott. He was only 2." Missy sniffed and wiped a tear away from her eye. "I'm sorry, I'm rambling."

"No, go ahead," Paul whispered.

"They were all riding together, on their way to the hospital to see me. I was about to be born. Then something went wrong with the tram. Right on a bridge, it skipped over the track, traveling at top speed. The tram flipped...Half the passengers were thrown from the tram when the emergency doors opened and they were tossed into the raging river...Days later, they found some of them down the river, but their lives had been stolen...

Others were never found...Like Daddy said, Mr. West, Mrs. West, their son...all three...Well, they never got to see me. But someone else was tossed from the tram that night, too, Paul."

Paul's mouth felt cottony. "Your brother, Scott."

Missy nodded. "So I've had to grow up without the brother I was supposed to have. It happened the day I was born. Daddy was the only one of the five that wasn't thrown out of the tram. He lost his best friends and a son that day. And I lost a brother. I lost him and there was nothing I could do about it."

"I didn't know."

"I know." Missy's makeup had faded with the moisture from her tears.

"I guess there's nothing either of us could do. In a way, you really do understand how I feel, don't you?"

"Don't give up your hope, Paul. I want you to find your family. I guess that's part of the reason I wanted to help...by helping you find your parents, I felt like I'd be able to somehow share in the joy...the joy of finding someone you never thought you'd get to know until you went to heaven—does that make any sense?"

Paul gently hugged Missy back and relaxed. It was over now—there was nothing more he knew to do.

Missy squinted and looked out the window.

"Paul, do you see that?"

"You mean the rain?" It was still pouring.

"No, I mean the building across the street."

Paul squinted, too, trying to make out the name on the sign atop the four-story building. Suddenly he gasped.

"You think that's a coincidence?"

"I don't think I believe in coincidences."

Missy shrieked, and in an instant both friends were up on their feet.

"Fiffer!" Paul cried. "Fiffer!"

The old man scuffled out from the back, carrying his broken baseball bat, ready to swing again. "What is it—is he back?"

"That expansion you plan on making across the street," Paul said, pointing out the window, "are you going to be moving into that building?"

"For goodness' sake, no," he responded. "That rat-infested tower is older than I am. It's coming down first."

"But you own it now?"

"Why, yes, I'm sorry to admit..."

"Can we look around?"

Mr. Fifopolis squinted. "Well, sure, but why on earth—"

"Thanks!" Paul shouted, heading for the door. "And will you please watch my bear for a few minutes?"

Fiffer nodded, but before he was able to say anything else, Paul and Missy had already bolted out the door.

Nautical Fabrics had been out of business for about nine years, and the faded welcome sign on the front entrance proved it. Nonetheless, it appeared as though the owners had left in a hurry because through the windows, Paul could see old, broken office furniture and tipped-over plastic plants scattered around each room.

"This is unbelievable!" Missy shouted through the plummeting rain. The two Superkids were rapidly getting soaked from head to toe. "I never even thought that the building would be here, let alone with stuff still inside. Paul, there could be records here of that blanket delivery to your mother—records that may include her name!"

"I wonder what Nautical Fabrics was in trouble for?" Paul said, peering in through the dirty glass. Missy shook her head.

"This place should be condemned and torn down. Look at the walls." Paul looked at the outside, wooden wall. It was splintered and fragile, as though it might crumble any second; a fire hazard waiting to happen. Then Paul looked over at a faded sticker posted on the front entrance.

"It *is* condemned," he realized, reading the sticker. "And Fiffer said it was ready to be torn down...Whoa!

Check out the date—this building is going to be torn down *tomorrow!*"

"Tomorrow?!" Missy was surprised. "This is some coincidence that we found it today!"

"If we're going to find a clue we have to get inside." Lightning flashed in the distance.

"Paul, I don't know. It doesn't look safe."

"I'll be extra careful!" Paul shouted, raindrops dripping off his nose. "I don't believe it's just a coincidence that we found this place one day before it'll be demolished. I'm going in!"

"Well, I'm staying out here!" Missy shouted back. "I think it looks too dangerous."

"Fine!"

"Fine!"

Paul pushed the door button, but nothing happened. As a second try, he grabbed the base of the window and pulled up. To his astonishment, the entire window came off in his hands. He almost dropped it. Juggling to keep his balance, Paul carefully set the window on the ground.

"I'll be back in 10 minutes," Paul promised. "Whether I find anything or not." Paul looked at Missy one last time before he entered. Her blond hair looked dark and thin, pulled down by the weight of the rain. It looked similar to how it had earlier that morning when she answered her bedroom door. Her makeup was faded, but evident. Her clothes, like his, were soaked. He appreciated all she was going through to help him. He knew now that this meant nearly as much to her as it did to him. Carefully, Paul lifted his leg over the window frame and entered the old building.

"And to think I could have been relaxing in the sun on Calypso Island right now..." Missy muttered.

Paul placed a foot on the ground and the floor creaked. He dropped in with his next step and his foot landed heavy—shoving it right through the floorboards.

Crack! "Ow!"

"Paul! You be careful!" Missy shouted from outside. Paul carefully pulled his foot out of the splintered wooden floor. He looked back.

"I'll be all right. But this place is really old." Paul continued his walk.

Halfway down the hall, Paul spotted a metal bulletin board. He walked over to it and read.

> ## WELCOME TO NAUTICAL FABRICS
> Lobby, Gift Shop,
> Public Restrooms . . . . . .Floor 1
>
> Administrative Offices
> and Special Orders . . . .Floor 2
>
> Records and Archives . .Floor 3
>
> Factory . . . . .Basement

Strange, Paul thought to himself, *I thought this was a four-story building.*

"Records and Archives" appeared to be Paul's best bet. He hoped Nautical Fabrics kept record of every blanket they gave away. Though he didn't know the exact day he was born, doctors told him it was probably near the middle of June—and as far as Paul was concerned that was good enough for him.

Now, if he could just locate the records of all the blankets given away in June the year he was born...

Paul looked for signs of stairs, knowing the elevator would be out, since it ran on electricity. The room was dark, but—unlike Fiffer's—the windows were large and there was enough light from outside to help Paul see where he was going. There probably would have been more light had it not had to filter through grime-covered glass.

There! An emergency door leading to fire stairs was off to Paul's left. He headed toward it, the excitement building in his mind as each step creaked. He reached the door and pushed. Pop! It opened and slid into the stairwell. Thick dust and garbage filled the stairway. A tinge of the musty smell hit Paul's nose and he winced. The pouring rain outside echoed in the stairwell, and Paul saw drops of water sneaking in through slim cracks in the structure. A small skylight let in enough light to illuminate Paul's way. He headed up the stairs, dodging a brave rat in the process.

At the third and top floor of the stairwell, Paul pushed open the emergency door. It opened reluctantly. As Paul looked in the room, he longed for his Academy gear—a flashlight, a compass, a med-pack and more. But all he had was his new Ashton Clothiers outfit—now extremely filthy and wet.

The Records and Archives floor was nothing but a wide room filled with row after row of filing cabinets, bookcases and stacks of boxes. Paul looked at his watch. He had less than five minutes to get back to Missy. He ran to the first filing cabinet on his left, shoved up against the wall. It was unmarked...and as Paul looked down the row, he realized they all were.

"Ugh! This could take all day!" he shouted to no one in particular. Paul opened the first drawer of the first cabinet. Inside were files labeled with six numbers—each dates! April first, second and third—26 years ago.

These must be records from when Nautical Fabrics began, Paul thought.

Paul pulled out a file at random. He flipped through it. Bank statements, customer letters, marketing materials and more sat inside. One paper that caught Paul's eye indicated a list of sales projections for the week ahead. The first half of the sheet listed 19 company names, the quantity of clothes they would receive and then the sales price. The second half of the sheet contained a list of 12 more company names, but each was completely marked out with thick, black marker. Paul was shocked at the expected sales prices on the second half of the sheet. *They had to be buying more than clothes,* he thought.

Then Paul found another paper. It was titled "Hospital Giveaways." Paul looked down the column and found the names of three hospitals. Under the name of each one, several women's names were listed. It was just what Paul was looking for.

Now he just had to find the right date. "Thank You, Father God, for giving me a spirit of wisdom and revelation," Paul whispered, counting on the truth in Ephesians 1:17.

Paul promptly replaced the folder and walked to a row of cabinets on the other side of the room. He was looking for the year he was born, somewhere around June. He planned on just taking the whole June stack. He pulled open another drawer at random. Paul was getting closer, he could feel it. He pulled out a folder dated May 11 of the year he turned 4. It contained another sheet titled "Hospital Giveaways" and a memo with more blotched out words. *Something must have been going on,* he thought. *Why else would they try to hide it with black marker?* He thought he could make out a few words underneath the marker—"ought," "total" and "CDD"—but it didn't make much sense. He refiled the folder.

Paul moved 10 filing cabinets back. He had to find that file with his mother's name! He pulled at a drawer. It wouldn't budge.

Paul pulled and yanked in short bursts, but the cabinet stayed tight. Frustrated, he kicked it hard with his shoe. The whole cabinet moved—backward. Paul kicked it again. It moved farther. With full force, Paul pushed the cabinet and it slid back. Suddenly, Paul found himself moving into a small room. He pushed the cabinet aside. Behind it, a flight of stairs ran upward with a door at the top.

I knew there were four floors, he pondered. Letting curiosity get the best of him, Paul headed up. The air was thick with dust and mildew. The rain still brushed the side and top of the building. Each step creaked as he rose—one step even broke through, weak from the combination of termites and time. At the top, he turned the old-fashioned doorknob. The door swung inward. A pack of rats scurried away.

The secret room was only about as big as Paul's dorm room at the Academy. Water dripped heavily from a skylight on the ceiling, and over time it had warped a desk and rusted a chair standing in the middle. The rest of the room was nothing to write home about. But what caught Paul's eye was the solitary box stashed in the far corner. Big, bold, red letters were marked on it, reading, "NME HQ—9 of 9. Ship Immediately."

The dust on the box and chewed-up corners indicated it had sat there quite awhile. Paul's instinct as a Superkid took over. He had to know what was inside. Step by careful step, Paul walked toward the cardboard box. He heard a rumble of thunder outside. Paul took off his watch and held it with the end of the metal band pointing outward. Methodically, he used it to slice open the taped box that never made its shipment. The sound of the ripping of the tape filled the room. Then Paul replaced his watch and pulled open the tabs.

Paul didn't know what to think when he saw what was inside. It was a tightly packed pile of red, yellow, blue and green fabric rolls. *Fabric?* Paul shook his head. He pulled out the blue one and it unfolded in his hands. It was a T-shirt, size L, with a stitched emblem on the front pocket that read, "NME." *Shirts for NME,* Paul thought. *Well, that's no crime.*

Paul tossed the blue shirt back in the box. But just before it hit its home, Paul saw the corner of something shining from beneath where the NME shirt had been placed.

What was that?

Paul picked up the blue shirt again and looked underneath. The edge of something golden and metallic shined from beneath the cloth. Paul reached in and pulled at it. The metal device was wrapped tightly in another T-shirt. Paul lifted it out. Carefully, he unwrapped the cloth from around the device.

Oh, no.

Paul couldn't believe his eyes. In his hands he was holding a Compound Destruction Device—a popular explosive used by NME. The CDD was powerful enough to destroy a large satellite or level a small building. *CDD...*Paul thought back to the blotched-out memo he read just moments earlier. One of the words Paul deciphered was "CDD." Paul gulped. CDDs were illegal to manufacture. Putting two and two together, Paul deduced that they must have been the reason Nautical Fabrics went out of business so quickly. The clothing business was only a front. Nautical Fabrics' real moneymaker was creating these small explosives and selling them to underground empires—like NME.

Paul looked at his watch. He had less than a minute to get back to Missy. Wrapping the CDD back up in the T-shirt, Paul was ready to shove it back in the box when a smell hit his nose.

It was the smell of liquor.

It was the same, putrid smell that trailed in after the thief entered Fiffer's only a while earlier.

"Looksie who I's found outside this here buildin'," a rough voice echoed in the room. When Paul turned around, he saw the angry thief standing in front of the only exit. Paul was so engrossed with the CDD, he didn't even hear him approaching. The thief's scruffy face was shiny with rainwater and sweat, and his clothes were sloshy-looking. In one hand he held his switchblade, now a dull red with Paul's blood. In the other hand, he held a beautiful, blond-haired prisoner by the neck of her jacket. Her big, blue eyes looked up at Paul, completely apologetic. Paul's heart grew heavy.

"I'm sorry," Missy whispered.

"It's not your fault," Paul said softly, acknowledging Missy's apology.

"Shuddup!" the pale-skinned thief cried. Then he took a step closer to Paul, dragging Missy with him. She winced at his strong grip. "Nobody messes wit me and gets way wit it," the thief spat at Paul. "Get you's hands up!"

Paul raised them immediately. All he could think about was Missy. *How can I free her? How can I save her?*

"Whazzat?!" the criminal shouted, pointing to the clothed CDD Paul was holding.

"It's—it's dangerous," Paul stated, wanting to be entirely honest.

"Yeah, it looks like a real scary sock."

"It's not a sock—it's a shirt. And it's what's inside that's dangerous."

"You's got a weapon? Izzat it?" the thief growled. The man pointed to a far wall with his switchblade. "Throw it o'er there! Throw it there now!"

"I don't think I should—"

"Do it!" the thief cried. He pulled his blade close to Missy's face. "Do it now!"

Trying to be as gentle as he could with the CDD, Paul set it on the ground. He wasn't sure if it was even active any more, but he didn't want to take the risk.

"There, I'm setting it down."

"I said over *there!*" the thief yelled, pointing to the side of the room. Then he lurched forward with his right foot first. Missy was swept along and Paul leapt back. The thief landed in front of the cloth-covered explosive device and kicked it hard in protest, unaware of the implications.

"Noooo!" Paul shouted. He closed his eyes and grabbed his ears as the CDD slammed against the far wall and bounced back to the center of the room. Fury grabbed hold of the armed man and he launched out kicking for the CDD again. "Don't!!!" Paul cried. This time the thief's kick slammed it against the desk. It ricocheted off the center of the desk and went barreling to the back of the room, flying out the open door and down the stairs. Paul's nerves cringed every time he heard it hit a step on the way down. Any hit could be the one to make it explode.

BOOM!

Paul's heart skipped a beat. But then he realized the boom he heard wasn't the sound of an explosion, but rather the CDD hitting a tin filing cabinet. He relaxed a bit. The CDD was quiet beyond the door, apparently having come to rest in the Records and Archives room.

Paul let out a sigh of relief—but not for long. The crazed man still had hold of Missy.

"Five minutes until detonation."

Paul and the thief looked at Missy.

"What?!" the thief asked, pulling her head back by her hair.

"I didn't say anything!" Missy objected. "It came from down there!"

"You's tryin' to trick me!" the thief shouted. "Not gonna work!"

"No—she's right," Paul interrupted. "It was from down there. It was the CDD. When you kicked it, you must have hit the timed detonation sequence. It's going to detonate in five minutes. We have to get out of here."

"What?!" the thief pressed. Hot, liquor-scented breath filtered out between his rotting teeth.

"It's a bomb, blockhead!" Missy shouted. "And it's going off in five minutes! *Let me go!*"

"SHUDDUP!" The strong man pulled at her hair with his meaty hands. Her whole head pulled back again with the pressure. Paul moved forward, but recoiled when the man lashed out again with his switchblade. Paul slid to the side, but once again the tip of the blade caught Paul's left hand. The blade slashed through the bandages Missy had wrapped, opening the wound.

"Yooooowwww!" Paul grabbed his wounded hand with his free one.

"Get you's hands up and don't try nuttin' else!"

Paul reluctantly obeyed.

"Four minutes until detonation."

"What are you going to do to us?" Missy pressed. Paul could tell she was weary.

"I's gonna teach you's what happens when you's mess wit me." He smiled a toothy, devilish smile and tossed Missy beside Paul. She hit the ground hard and Paul could hear the old, wooden floor crack beneath her. The man raised his switchblade.

In a split second, thoughts dashed through Paul's mind and feelings raced through his body like fire on a strip of gasoline. *How will we ever make it out of this alive? How do I protect Missy? What can I do? We have no protection. We have no weapons. We have no hope.*

You have more *than hope,* the Holy Spirit spoke up inside Paul's spirit. It was as clear as the thunder in the sky outside. *Look at your hands.*

Without a moment's hesitation, Paul obeyed the urging in his spirit and glanced at his hands—the wounded one first, then the other. There they were, both raised at his side and bloodstained. Paul's thoughts immediately flashed back to his vision: a figure with outstretched, bloodstained hands. A figure whose hands and feet were nailed to a cross. A figure who took Paul's jacket and replaced it with a robe and with armor. A figure who replaced Paul's weapons with a sword and a shield. It was the making of a covenant—an agreement that couldn't be broken. A covenant—a real promise

made years ago when He changed places with Paul and
died on a real cross. A covenant with the creator of the
universe...a covenant with—

"Jesus," Paul spoke softly, feeling the spiritual armor
protecting his body. At once, as the thief's switchblade
came down on Paul's arm, the knife snapped in half,
flipping the metal blade onto the floor. The thief roared
and jumped back in surprise.

"Jesus," Paul spoke confidently this time, trusting in
the spiritual sword and shield he wore. The dirty man
took a step back in reflex, looking confused and scared.
Paul pointed his finger at the man and by the look on the
thief's face, he could tell the man was seeing the finger
of God Himself.

"No weapon that is used against me will defeat me,"
Paul prophesied, quoting Isaiah 54:17. "My victory
comes from the Lord!"

"Get-get-get-getta way from me!" The thief spat,
shaking his head and trembling.

Boldly, Paul began to quote scriptures from Psalm 91.
"In the Name of Jesus, I will not fear any danger by
night or an arrow during the day. I will not be hurt! For
the Lord is my protection. I have made God Most High
my place of safety. He has put His angels in charge of
me to watch over me wherever I go!"

The thief spun around dizzily and ran out the door,
screaming, "I don't want anything to do with you!" As
he hit the doorway, he tossed Missy's gold necklace

back into the room. Paul heard him smashing the unstable, wooden floor as he ran down the stairs and out the build-ing. Paul turned around and looked at Missy.

"You all right?" he asked, offering a hand. He could still feel the adrenaline running through his veins. Missy cracked a smile.

"You've really been paying attention during our morn-ing devotional times, haven't you?"

Paul nodded.

"Three minutes until detonation."

"We've gotta get out of here, Missy." Paul helped his friend up. She squeezed his hand, whispered a soft "thank you," and then headed, full force, for the door, not letting go of Paul. On the way out, she snatched her necklace off the ground and stuffed it in her pocket.

Paul moved in front of her as they headed down the steps. He worked to rush them through, while carefully avoiding the pitted impressions created by the thief when he ran out. In the Records and Archives room, the two Superkids hopped over the ticking time bomb reading "2:43."

Paul led Missy out into the stairwell and down to the first level. They made it halfway to the front door when Paul froze and Missy smashed into him.

"Oomph!"

"What are you stopping for?! Paul, we've only got a couple minutes!"

"The file. I've got to go get the file! I've got enough time—I'll meet you across the street! Go! This is my last chance to find out about my parents!"

Missy's eyes began to glass up. Paul smiled. "I'll be OK—really." Missy took a deep breath and let go of his hand. She took off toward the front door and Paul ran back to the stairs.

The sound of Missy's startled scream made Paul whip back around. His first thought was that the thief had returned...but what he saw was worse.

A heavy step by Missy had sent her down into the splintering floor. The bending of her knees kept her from falling through, and she was struggling to get out. Paul watched as she pulled herself up—and then the floorboards snapped and she fell down farther. She was stuck up to her waist.

Paul could hear his own heart pumping. He headed for Missy. She needed help.

"No! Paul! Go get your file! I'll be all right! This is your only chance! When that bomb goes off, this building's coming down—and you'll never find your answer."

Paul didn't heed her word or hesitate. He ran straight to her, secured his footing and grabbed her hands. He pulled and she kicked, trying to get clear. Floorboards splintered and creaked, crying out to be free.

"Paul, leave me! This is your only chance!"

"You came all the way down here for me because I needed help! That's what family does: We help each other!

I see it now! Through the covenant, we're brother and sister! *You're* my family! *You're* part of that second half I've been missing! I won't let you go!"

"But Paul—if you don't go get that file now, you'll never find your real family!"

"Missy," Paul shouted, looking straight into her eyes, *"you're* my real family! I'm not willing to risk your life, hoping that I'll find some family I never had! You and Rapper and Val and Alex and Commander Kellie —you're my family now!"

With a tug and a scream, Paul pulled Missy clear of the hole. She tumbled down, then quickly stood back up.

"Let's get out of here!" Paul cried. "It's going to blow any second!"

The two friends hurdled through the window opening and dashed toward the street.

Ka-BOOOOOOOOMMM!!! BOOM! BOOM! BOOM!

Paul and Missy were flung through the air and the rain as the explosion blasted from the building. They hit the ground 15 feet from where they were last standing. Hot rain, wood and glass poured from the sky, littering the earth around the fallen Superkids. Lying on their stomachs, they covered their heads for protection. Paul glanced back long enough to see the fourth floor cave in on the third, taking with it hundreds of exploded filing cabinets and thousands of burning files. The old paper and rotting wood caused the building to burn down at a fast pace.

Paul looked one last time at his dream, burning away, turning to rubble. It had all seemed so right—finding the clues, running into one coincidence after another. But now it seemed so useless.

A lone piece of paper drifted down from above, swinging in the wind. Then, weighted by the rainwater, it dropped quickly beside Paul. Missy leaned up with him when they saw the words across the top that proclaimed, "Hospital Giveaways." Paul snatched the paper off the ground and his finger flowed down the paper. Three hospital names. Twenty-five patients who received free blankets.

"I'm sorry," Missy whispered. Paul looked at her, questioning. She pointed at the date. It was from June 18...but six years before Paul was born. Paul crumpled up the paper in disgust and sent it sailing through the air. He smashed a muddy puddle with his fist in disgust. Coincidence had gotten him nowhere.

Paul looked up to see a figure dressed in a glowing, white robe coming toward him. His face was bright, too—and his eyes were piercing, like a beam of sunlight reflecting off a polished metal surface. Paul felt a gripping at his heart and the force of peace at the same time.

The figure promptly removed his robe and traded it with the light-gray jacket Paul wore. On Paul, the robe glistened like no garment he'd ever seen. Next, the man produced a full suit of armor, similar to a knight's armor. He clipped the breastplate onto Paul, followed by the lower-body part and then the shoes. He placed the helmet on Paul's head and handed him a glistening sword and shield set.

"The agreement must be sealed," the figure stated, his voice booming like thunder. Suddenly, as Paul stood frozen, a rugged, wooden cross rose behind the man. Without even a blink of hesitation, he stretched out his arms parallel to the structure's crossbeam. Wearing Paul's thin jacket, he was easily bound to the cross.

Paul couldn't bear to watch as he saw nails appear in the figure's hands and feet. The man cried out, and Paul could do nothing.

Paul was speechless, but eventually the words came. "Why would you give me all this? Why are you going through this? Why—when you wouldn't have to?"

With a soft look of love on His face, the Figure smiled with strength and responded, "I've gone through all this for you, Paul. I've gone through all this because I wanted you as a part of My family."

Paul awoke with a start.

▲ ▲ ▲

After a long hard nap, Paul faced the evening with mixed emotions. On one hand, he was thrilled that his painful adventure was over. On the other hand, it also left him unsettled that he wasn't even one step closer to the answer of finding his real parents than he was when he left Superkid Academy two days ago.

But something new was born inside Paul. Suddenly he had a realization—a revelation he had never truly understood before. He *did* have a family. When he made Jesus the Lord of His life almost four years ago, Paul didn't know it. But that day, he was adopted by God—adopted into His family. Now he had a family who cared for him, loved him and wanted the best for him. He had a family because of Jesus' sacrifice. And other Christians, other children of God, were his new brothers and sisters.

Paul was no longer the poor orphan from Sawyer. Now he was a child of God—a son because of a covenant made in blood. Paul realized that, like any other Christian, he had the right to share in the blessings of that covenant —health, prosperity, strength and help. The awareness hit Paul like a blast of fire: He had exchanged his weaknesses, insecurities and faults for the Lord's strength, armor and weapons against the enemy. Paul finally understood what it meant to be born again!

Paul thought about this as he and Missy were reclining in the Ashton's living room with Mr. and Mrs. Ashton. Missy's parents sat comfortably, holding hands, on their plush couch, and Paul and Missy each occupied one of the Victorian chairs in front of the fireplace. Missy leaned back, with her legs outstretched, welcoming the peace and quiet. Her blond hair was straight today, as she had styled it, curled in on the sides toward her soft facial features. It was the same style her mother had worn two days before.

Mr. and Mrs. Ashton were in their social attire; Gregg Ashton with a button-down shirt and slacks, and Lois Ashton with a silk blouse and a flowery, silk skirt.

Paul was in a clean pair of bluejeans and another Ashton Clothiers rugby, this time solid navy blue. Paul's legs ached (though he imagined Missy's ached even more from her fall) and his hand was bandaged. It was healing rapidly; he could tell already.

"That's some adventure!" Gregg Ashton conceded after listening to Paul and Missy's lively account of the story.

"I'm just glad you two are all right," Lois Ashton added. "And I hope that criminal is put behind bars— threatening my Tootle like that."

"He already is," her husband assured. "I made sure of that. Good for us, the police were already in the area since Mr. Fifopolis had called them. They caught that scoundrel as he ran from the building." Mr. Ashton's eyebrows bobbed up and down when he said the word "scoundrel."

"We're going to go visit him in jail tomorrow," Paul threw in. "Now that he's seen the power of God firsthand, maybe he'll be more open to making Jesus *his* Lord, too."

"Well, no more adventure for *me* this vacation." Missy threw her hands out as she delivered her ultimatum. "Yesterday I had enough knives and explosions and stinky-breath criminals for an entire year." Paul laughed out loud. Then she added, "And to think that I could have been relaxing in the sun on Calypso Island."

Paul toyed with pointing out that it was her decision to come, but he decided against it. He knew she joined him because she cared. And, ultimately, she wouldn't have had it any other way.

"Still," Mr. Ashton surmised, "it's too bad the clues leading to your family fizzled out. I was really hoping you'd find them."

Paul slowly stood up from the Victorian chair and stretched his weary bones. He moved over to the fireplace and looked at the shrine of Missy pictures.

"I was, too," Paul admitted. "But I've learned something." Paul picked up the picture of Missy in her beauty pageant, leaned against the mantle and ran his thumb along the frame. "I've learned that I have a family with a bond that's even stronger than flesh and blood. You guys, the other Superkids, even people I have yet to meet. We're all brothers and sisters. We're all family and we all share in the blessings God has given to us. This revelation filled the second half of my life that I'd always been missing. It showed me the truth."

Paul set the picture back on the mantle.

Missy's mother was holding Paul's bear and blanket. "You know, the one thing that's funny about this blanket are the letters under the word 'Nautical.' It says 'SA 17 36.'"

"I've always thought it was just 'USA' and a ZIP code," Paul admitted. Mrs. Ashton nodded.

"Hey, look at this!" Paul shouted, picking up the picture of Missy as a baby. She was leaning on a yellow ramp. Her bottom lip was sticking out in protest. "Boy, Missy, you're not really living up to that 'Tootle' name here, are ya?"

Lois Ashton chuckled. "Actually, Paul, that's our son, Scott. Did you know Missy had an older brother?"

"Oh, I'm sorry," Paul felt embarrassed. "Yeah, she told me."

"It's all right," Gregg Ashton comforted. "They looked just alike, didn't they?"

Paul spied the picture again. "You're not kidding."

"Oh my gosh! That's it!" Missy cried. "The letters 'SA' stand for Scott Ashton! You're Scott Ashton—my long-lost brother!"

Missy's mother scrunched up her face. "I think that may be a bit of a stretch, Tootle. You and Paul don't really look alike."

Missy shrugged. "We both have blond hair..." Mr. Ashton shook his head, smirking. "Well," Missy finally admitted, "it would have made an interesting story, anyway."

"Now this cute one must be your brother, then, too," Paul said, lifting up the large, framed picture of a couple holding the baby. "Check it out!" Paul suddenly shouted, pointing to the photo. "That's one of Fiffer's bears!"

Missy slid off her chair and clunked herself in the head with a finger. "I knew I'd seen one somewhere before. It must have been—" Missy stopped speaking.

"What?" Paul asked.

"That...that's not Scott or me, Paul. That's a picture of the Wests—Daddy's best friend and his wife with their son...before the accident."

Mrs. Ashton's blue eyes drew to the ground.

"I'm sorry," Paul apologized again. "I'm, uh, really striking out here...I'm sorry." The Wests were a tall couple and their baby took after their stature. He was long and crying, not happy at all that a big bear was coming at him. Paul scratched at the glass on the picture.

"There's a...smudge of something on the glass."

"That's not a smudge," Missy observed, looking at the picture. A small mark in the shape of a crescent moon drew from the baby's lower calf to the top of his foot. Missy lifted the picture from Paul's hands. "See, that's just a birthmark."

Paul's stomach squeezed into a tight knot and the color drained from his face. His ears rang and his body became hot in an instant.

"Paul! What is it?!" Missy shouted, noticing his sudden change in complexion. "What's wrong?"

"Paul?" Missy's father questioned, leaning forward. But Paul waved his hands in front of himself, shooing them away.

Sinking back down onto his Victorian chair, Paul, speechless and weak, grabbed onto his left sock—and he pushed it down.

The sock crumpled, revealing the middle of Paul's calf...and the crescent-shaped birthmark that ran down from mid-calf to the top of his foot.

Mrs. Ashton's head snapped up and her chin quivered. Mr. Ashton sat stunned and immobile. Missy's mouth just dropped. Suddenly it all fell into place. The foggy night. The families traveling together to the hospital to visit a mother who was about to give birth. The tram skipping the track. The emergency doors opening, mercilessly tossing passengers—including a baby boy—out into a raging river. A passerby who discovered him a couple days later and, thinking he was abandoned by his parents, brought him to the nearby, small-town orphanage. An orphanage caretaker who received the baby, bruised from the crash, and assumed it was from an unloving family.

Missy clutched onto the picture with both hands and compared the birthmarks. They were identical. She pulled the picture to her chest and cuddled it tightly with crossed arms. A tear of amazement crawled down her cheek as she blurted out the only thing that came to mind.

"They're your—they're your—they're your—they're your—they're your—"

"They're my..." Paul choked. He could barely say the word. "...parents. They're my *parents!*"

Paul jumped up, still feeling weak, but full of strength at the same time. He threw his arms around Missy and squeezed tight. "My *parents,*" he whimpered through tears he couldn't hold back. "I finally found my parents!" Both his face and Missy's were tear-stained when they let go of one another. Then Paul looked at Mrs. Ashton. Her mascara had run and her hands were still over her mouth in disbelief. Fighting to breathe between sobs, she slowly stood and grabbed hold of Paul.

"Paul," she whispered, "if only we'd known you were alive..." Paul's arms tightened around her, wrinkling her silk blouse. Hugging her, knowing she had known his parents—known him—long ago, was the strangest feeling. Mr. Ashton stood up and looked at Paul. His face held the attributes of sheer shock. He moved closer and Mrs. Ashton released her embrace. Paul looked at Mr. Ashton and he looked at Paul.

The gentle man put out his arms and placed his hands on Paul's shoulders, keeping Paul at arm's length. He stared straight into Paul's brown eyes with his own, searching. "Your father and I had a covenant," Mr. Ashton began. Paul could feel warm tears rolling down his cheeks. "Our covenant was like David and Jonathan's in the Bible. We were best friends.

"I remember in the Bible, in 2 Samuel 9, after Jonathan had died, David found out someone related to Jonathan was still alive. That man was named Mephibosheth and he lived in a place called Lo-debar. Lo-debar means 'desolate place.'"

"I've been there," Paul chuckled and sniffed at the same time.

"For 14 years you have," Mr. Ashton agreed. "When David discovered Mephibosheth was still alive, he let him become like part of his family. Paul..."

Paul could feel the lump in his throat aching.

"Today, as far as I'm concerned, in Christ, you're a part of this family. What we have is yours."

"But I don't have hardly anything to give back," Paul said softly.

"You can give us you," Mr. Ashton offered, his voice cracking. "You are a part of our family from now on. You're welcome to call this place home whenever you want. What's ours, my covenant son, is yours." Gregg

Ashton began to cry. He pulled Paul close to him and hugged him tightly, his chest reverberating with soft sobs.

After a long moment, Paul and the Ashtons all sat down again. Missy reached over and grabbed Paul's hand. Her hand was warm as she squeaked out, "I had a brother stolen from me the day I was born...but today..." Missy couldn't finish her sentence. But she didn't need to. Paul knew what she was feeling, because he was feeling the same thing.

This family he had wasn't the family he was born to, nor was he the son born to them. But today, God knitted them together like four strings making up one strong rope, fulfilling a desire in each of their hearts. For promises, for love and for family.

▲   ▲   ▲

An hour later, after emotions came to rest and solemnness set in, something hit Paul that he had almost missed.

"I've got it," he said.

"You've got what?" Mr. Ashton asked.

"Second Samuel 9—that's the scripture you said earlier, right?"

"Yes..."

"Well, the blanket says, 'SA 17 36.' What if that's an abbreviation for a Bible verse?"

The room fell silent. All at once, they all jumped up and ran to the kitchen to pick up the Bible. Mr. Ashton had it first. He flipped to 2 Samuel 17. The three others looked on excitedly as he ran his finger down the verses.

"There's only 29 verses," Lois Ashton pointed out.

"First Samuel! Look at the first book of Samuel!" Missy cried.

Mr. Ashton flipped back hurriedly. "Here it is!" he announced. He read. "David said, 'Your servant has killed both the lion and the bear.'"

Everyone looked at each other, blank-faced. Paul shook his head. "That doesn't make any—"

Suddenly Mrs. Ashton darted out of the room. The crew shot out after her.

"What, Mommy? What?" Missy shouted.

They followed her back into the living room. She grabbed Paul's stuffed animal and held it out, its sewn-up tummy sticking out. "The bear!" she announced, wide-eyed. A smile broke out on Paul's face. Mr. Ashton's lips turned up. Missy looked a bit confused.

"What about it?" she wondered.

"The scripture said David killed a bear," her mom explained. "I think that's what we need to do."

"What?!" Paul could tell Missy still didn't understand. But he did. And apparently her husband did, too, because he was already handing her a pair of scissors. Mrs. Ashton grabbed them and began slicing away at the sewing marks on the bear's belly.

"Ugggg!" Missy cried. "My mommy, 'The Bear-killer!' My mommy, 'The—' Oh! Good thinking!"

The stuffed stomach of the bear popped open when she cut the last sewn thread. Lying there, encased in the layers of cotton and filling was a small, plastic tube. Paul carefully pulled it out. When he popped open the tube, a tiny, silver device wrapped in gray paper dropped out. It was labeled, 'For our son.'

"It's a holo-cartridge," Mr. Ashton observed. "I'll be right back."

Paul rolled it around in his hand. A holo-cartridge was like a small roll of film, but it had the ability to contain an actual holographic recording. To watch it, all you needed was a holographic projector. A moment later, Missy's father returned with one.

They all sat down again, but each of them, especially Paul, were on the edge of their seats. Paul dropped the small container into the projector.

A sizzling sound filled the room and then suddenly an electronic picture emerged. Two three-dimensional figures stood in the center of the room, looking straight at Paul. He knew immediately who they were. They looked just like him.

"Hey, guy!" the male image greeted. "It's me, your dad, Evans West and this is your mom, Lynda."

The woman giggled and playfully jabbed the man in the side whispering, "He knows who we are!" They both laughed.

The woman waved at Paul. He couldn't help but wave back even though it was a recording. There they stood—his parents—before him. They were dressed nicely, his father in a pressed shirt, slacks and a tie. His mother wore a flowered dress and white shoes. His skin was slightly ruddy, like Paul's. Hers was a soft white. Paul had his father's nose and mouth...and his mother's eyes. His hair was short and dark. Hers was long and wavy blond. They were beautiful.

"That's you in there," Paul's dad said, pointing to his mother's stomach. "We just found out you were in there today, so we wanted to make this holo-film for you. Kind of goofy, huh?"

Paul slightly shook his head as he was absorbed in watching them move.

"We don't even know what your name will be yet," Mr. West said, "but we want you to know more than anything that we love you."

"We love you very much," his mother agreed. Paul felt like crying again.

"And if anything should ever happen to us, we want you to know you've still got a family. All around you are brothers and sisters, and God, your Father, Who loves you more than she or I or any person ever could. Of course, you still have us. We'll be in heaven, cheering you on. And we'll be waiting for you, Son. Because one day, you'll be coming home, too. And then we'll see you again for eternity...face to face."

The woman waved. The man smiled. It was Paul's smile. And the holo-film ended.

"What did they end up naming me?" Paul asked the Ashtons after several silent minutes had passed.

Mr. Ashton fielded the question. "Thomas," he said. "Thomas West."

"Thomas Thomas West?" Paul asked.

Mrs. Ashton chuckled. "Just 'Thomas West.' They never gave you a middle name."

Paul pondered the new name in his mind. "Then I'll go by Thomas Paul West. I'll still be Paul to my friends...but I finally have a full name...a *real* full name. 'Thomas Paul West.' *'Paul West.'"*

He liked the way it sounded. It was perfect.

"There's just one more thing," Missy interjected. "This paper that was wrapped around the holo-film—it has some writing on the other side."

Mr. Ashton looked at it and began to chuckle.

"What is it?" Paul asked.

"This is a certificate of ownership," Missy's dad answered. "I never knew."

Mrs. Ashton looked at her husband quizzically. He answered her unspoken question. "Paul, your father was one of the investors in Ashton Clothiers. He never told me."

"What does that mean?" Paul wondered. "Are you saying—"

"I'm saying, when you turn 21, you've got quite an inheritance coming."

Mr. Ashton laughed. Then Mrs. Ashton and Missy joined in. And finally Paul did, too.

Paul stayed up late into the night watching the holo-film over and over. He finally found his parents. He finally got to see them. He wouldn't meet them for years to come, but he could live with that. He knew where they were and he loved them. And he knew they loved him, too.

Now, on earth, his parents had left him a legacy. In addition to an inheritance, he had gained a family that cared for him as though he was their own. He could tell they felt blessed, for they looked at Paul in a new light. He was like a son to them. And he knew Missy felt blessed, because she found someone who would be like a brother. But Paul knew, without a doubt, that today he was the most blessed of all. For in a matter of moments, he had inherited a covenant father, mother and sister that he could love with all his heart. Moreover, he'd also received a revelation about the kingdom of God—about an even *larger* family and the blessings that came with it. And, these blessings, Paul was confident, he would never lose again.

Early the next morning, Paul and Missy placed a call to Superkid Academy. They had to let their friends and their commander know about the powerful revelation they had discovered.

"Hello, Superkids!" Commander Kellie shouted as her face lit up on the ComPhone display. "It's good to hear from you!"

Immediately, Paul and Missy told her about all the extraordinary things that had happened to them: from the wayward footlocker ride to the exploding building to the final discovery of Paul's family. Their commander was thrilled for them and told them how she looked forward to their safe return. As the details of their adventure came to a close, she turned noticeably tense on the view screen.

"What is it, Commander Kellie?" Paul wondered. "Is something wrong?"

Missy apologized immediately. "I'm sorry for stowing away, Commander. I just had to come—but now I realize that the way I did it was wrong. You can assign me to bathroom cleanup, if needed."

"We'll deal with that later," Commander Kellie said. "Right now there's something much more serious."

Missy wiped her forehead playfully. "Whew!" she kidded. "Well, maybe I should just pick my own punishment then. After all, I could break a nail on that hard bathroom floor. Maybe I should be sentenced to 30 days of nonstop shopping. Oh, no! Not that! Anything but that! OK, if you must. I think that's a fair punishment."

The commander didn't crack a smile.

"Something's really wrong, isn't it?" Missy finally reasoned.

"It's Rapper and Valerie," Commander Kellie stated.

Paul looked at Missy and Missy looked at Paul. "Did they finally get to Calypso Island?" Paul asked.

"They did," Commander Kellie said flatly, "but that's the problem. They flew into a heavy storm and were forced to land."

"Yeah..." Missy was listening with all sincerity now.

"Well," the commander continued, "we have a serious problem. It seems that Valerie is nowhere to be found."

"What are you saying?" Missy pressed. Valerie was her best friend.

Commander Kellie let out a long, slow breath. "We need to start praying right now," she ordered. "Something has happened to Valerie."

To be continued...

When Valerie is **abandoned** on a hostile island,
she discovers she's **not** alone!

Look for *Commander Kellie and the Superkids*SM
novel #3—

Escape From Jungle Island

by Christopher P.N. Maselli

Available from Heirborne™!

Prayer for Salvation

Father God, I believe that Jesus is Your Son and that You raised Him from the dead for me. Jesus, I give my life to You. Right now, I make You the Lord of my life and choose to follow You forever. I love You and I know You love me. Thank You, Jesus, for giving me a new life. Thank You for coming into my heart and being my Savior. I am a child of God! Amen.

About the Author

Christopher P.N. Maselli is the author of the *Commander Kellie and the Superkids* series. He also writes the bimonthly children's magazine, *Shout! The Voice of Victory for Kids,* and has contributed to the *Commander Kellie and the Superkids* movies.

Originally from Iowa and a graduate of Oral Roberts University, Chris now lives with his wife, Gena, in Fort Worth, Texas, where he is actively involved in the children's ministry at his local church. When he's not writing, he enjoys in-line skating, playing computer games and collecting Legos.

Other Books Available

Baby Praise Board Book
Noah's Ark Coloring Book
The Shout! Super-Activity Book

***Commander Kellie and the Superkids_{SM}* Books:**

The SWORD Adventure Book
Commander Kellie and the Superkids_{SM}
    Preteen Novels by Christopher P.N. Maselli

    #1 *The Mysterious Presence*
    #2 *The Quest for the Second Half*
    #3 *Escape From Jungle Island*
    #4 *In Pursuit of the Enemy*

World Offices
of Kenneth Copeland Ministries

For more information about KCM and a free
catalog, please write the office nearest you:

Kenneth Copeland Ministries
Fort Worth, Texas 76192-0001

Kenneth Copeland
Locked Bag 2600
Mansfield Delivery Centre
QUEENSLAND 4122
AUSTRALIA

Kenneth Copeland
Post Office Box 15
BATH
BA1 1GD
ENGLAND

Kenneth Copeland
Private Bag X 909
FONTAINEBLEAU
2032
REPUBLIC OF SOUTH AFRICA

Kenneth Copeland
Post Office Box 378
Surrey
BRITISH COLUMBIA
V3T 5B6
CANADA

UKRAINE
L'VIV 290000
Post Office Box 84
Kenneth Copeland Ministries
L'VIV 290000
UKRAINE

We're Here for You!

Shout! ...The dynamic magazine just for kids!

Shout! The Voice of Victory for Kids is a Bible-charged, action-packed, bimonthly magazine available FREE to kids everywhere! Featuring *Wichita Slim* and *Commander Kellie and the Superkids*, *Shout!* is filled with colorful adventure comics, challenging games and puzzles, exciting short stories, solve-it-yourself mysteries and much more!!

Stand up, sign up and get ready to *Shout!*

Believer's Voice of Victory Television Broadcast

Join Kenneth and Gloria Copeland, and the *Believer's Voice of Victory* broadcasts, Monday through Friday and on Sunday each week, and learn how faith in God's Word can take your life from ordinary to extraordinary. This is some of the best teaching you'll ever hear, designed to get you where you want to be—*on top!*

You can catch the *Believer's Voice of Victory* broadcast on your local, cable or satellite channels.

*Check your local listings for times and stations in your area.

Believer's Voice of Victory Magazine

Enjoy inspired teaching and encouragement from Kenneth and Gloria Copeland each month in the *Believer's Voice of Victory* magazine. Also included are real-life testimonies of God's miraculous power and divine intervention into the lives of people just like you!

It's more than just a magazine—it's a ministry.

If you or some of your friends would like to receive a FREE subscription to *Shout!,* just send each kid's name, date of birth and complete address to:

Kenneth Copeland Ministries
Fort Worth, Texas 76192-0001
Or call:
1-800-359-0075
(9 a.m.-5 p.m. CT)

The Harrison House Vision

Proclaiming the truth and the power
Of the Gospel of Jesus Christ
With excellence;

Challenging Christians to
Live victoriously,
Grow spiritually,
Know God intimately.